Based on the *Barnyard* movie by Nickelodeon Movies and Paramount Pictures

SIMON SPOTLIGHT
An imprint of Simon & Schuster Children's Publishing Division
1230 Avenue of the Americas, New York, New York 10020
© 2006 by Paramount Pictures Corporation and Viacom International Inc.
All Rights Reserved. Nickelodeon, Nickelodeon Barnyard and all related titles, logos and characters are trademarks of Viacom International Inc.
SIMON SPOTLIGHT and colophon are registered trademarks of Simon & Schuster, Inc.
Manufactured in the United States of America
First Edition 10 9 8 7 6 5 4 3 2 1
ISBN-13: 978-1-4169-0722-0
ISBN-10: 1-4169-0722-X

BARNYARD

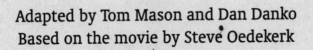

Adapted by Tom Mason and Dan Danko
Based on the movie by Steve Oedekerk

Simon Spotlight/Nickelodeon Movies
New York   London   Toronto   Sydney

One

"Good morning, Duke!" The farmhouse door flung open, squeaking on its rusty hinges as a short, squat farmer bounded down the creaky, wooden steps. His hat rested very low on his head, nearly covering his eyes. His enormous, round nose popped from his face like a lightbulb. With a goofy smile on his face, he waddled toward the coop, a bucket of chicken feed in his hand.

Duke, the farmer's faithful canine of many dog years, barked happily as he raced around the corner and jumped on his owner, licking his face. The farmer

5

rubbed Duke's head. Then he pulled a bone from the back pocket of his overalls and tossed it across the yard. Duke took off after it, loping across the dew-covered lawn, the wet grass sticking to his paws.

The farmer looked around. The old pot-bellied mule leaned up against a bale of hay. Cows and sheep grazed in the field. Chickens pecked at the ground. A rooster strutted across the yard. It was another morning in the barnyard.

"I'm just headin' out to the fields, Duke," the farmer called out to his loyal companion. "I'll be back." He patted Duke on the head once more and climbed into his rickety pickup truck. The engine revved and puffed smoke from the exhaust as the farmer drove off down the dirt road.

All of the animals in the barnyard froze. The air was still enough to hear a straw of hay drop. The sheep gathered on the hillside to watch the truck disappear into the horizon. Then one of the sheep poked his head out from the herd.

"Clear!" the sheep yelled. A sigh of relief washed over the animals. The sheep stood up on his back legs and stretched his arms up high, like a cat waking up from its nap. The other sheep followed suit, giving their hind legs and arms a nice, big stretch.

One by one, the other barnyard animals popped up on their legs and began stretching out their backs. Cows shook out their arms and tried to get the creaks out of their necks. Sheep jogged in place to loosen up their muscles. Miles, the old pot-bellied mule, stood up and scratched his ears, and after a good stretch, the chickens picked their feed up off the ground and began eating like civilized folk. Pig, the pig, stood up and stretched his legs and back. Then he plopped face down onto a big puddle of mud.

The shadow of a big cow fell over the ground. It was Ben, strolling through the yard on his way to the barn. His two hind legs carried his massive frame with ease.

"Morning, Ben," greeted Miles. As Ben passed by, Miles stuck his hind leg back, slid a clipboard out from under the hay, kicked it up into the air, and watched as it sailed straight into Ben's hooves.

"Thanks, Miles," Ben said. "Let me know if you see Otis."

"Oh, I'm staying out of that one," Miles replied with a chuckle. The old mule knew better than to stick his scruffy ears into that mess.

Ben smirked and tucked the clipboard under his arm. "Okay," he announced in a stern voice. "Meeting's in five minutes, and I want *everyone* present."

7

"Duke, have you seen Otis?" Ben asked as he passed the dog.

"Nope, I haven't seen him," Duke answered. "Now, where was I? Oh yeah." Suddenly remembering, he got down on all fours and continued sniffing his fellow animals.

Ben sighed and continued walking toward the barn when he heard laughter beyond the wooden fence that marked the boundary of the barnyard. He looked toward the sound. There they were, the Jersey cows: Eddy, Igg, and Bud. They were propped up against the fence as if they didn't have a care in the world. And they didn't. These outcasts wouldn't be caught dead at the morning meeting or doing anything productive at all, for that matter. Eddy, Igg, and Bud were tough heifers with thick leather hides, branding tattoos, and tags that hung like earrings. As far as Ben was concerned, the Jersey cows were trouble.

"Hey, Benny boy huh," Eddy said in his thick Jersey accent. "Hey, uh you seen Otis around?"

"Yes," Ben lied. "I know exactly where Otis is. You boys just steer clear of Otis, all right?"

"Aw, anything you say there, Ben," Eddy said. "But, uh, we'll take a rain check on that meeting, though."

"Yeah, a rain check," Igg agreed.

"Yeah, that, huh," Bud added. "Check."

Eddy, Igg, and Bud hopped the fence and strolled off down the hill. They laughed and elbowed one another as they left.

Ben shook his head. The truth was that he didn't know where his son, Otis, was. Etta, a hen, strolled past with a group of chicks. "Etta, have you seen Otis?" Ben whispered.

"Oh, Ben, don't worry," she replied. "I'm sure he's heading for the meeting right now."

The look on Ben's face said he didn't quite believe her.

"All right boys, here's the dealio," Otis said. All of Otis's closest pals had gathered to watch this amazing new sport he had discovered. No, Otis wasn't exactly heading for the morning meeting. Instead the easygoing cow was goofing off as usual.

High on top of a huge hill, the carefree cow teetered on a surfboard strapped to a block of ice and stared down onto a makeshift ski slope. The only thing keeping the ice cube from sliding backward over the cliff was a small branch from an apple tree. "It's a little creation of mine I like to call Hill Surfing. Now let me break it down for you: You got your hill. You got your surfing. You got your, uh, completion of the breakdown!" he concluded.

"Okay, it's go time!" Otis said excitedly.

"I'll try it, I'm down," cried Otis's best friend, Pip, a mouse tiny in stature only. Pip jumped onto Otis's shoulder and prepared for takeoff. "Shotgun!"

"Piggy-back!" yelled Pig, raising his hand to be second in line.

"Never," announced Peck, the naive rooster. "You are all gonna die." Suddenly, Peck noticed his friend Freddy, the good-hearted ferret, creeping awfully close. Then Freddy began sniffing his friend.

It was hard for Freddy to be friends with a rooster. His thoughts wandered as he inhaled his friend's delicious scent. What a good friend Peck had always been—a very, very good and tasty friend with a yummy neck, plump belly. . . . A few simple spices and some barbecue sauce could really bring out the flavor of—

"Freddy!" Peck said, trying to snap his friend out of another daydream.

"Nothing!" Freddy cried nervously, pretending he wasn't sniffing anything.

"Wup, wait a second, photo-op," Otis exclaimed.

At that, Peck, Freddy, and Pig all jumped onto the surfboard to pose. A gopher popped up and took their picture. The gophers had a habit of collecting and selling human paraphernalia.

Suddenly, Otis noticed that Pig was eating an apple.

"Hey, Pig, where'd you get that apple?"

"This apple? It was originally attached to this," he answered, holding up the very same apple branch that was keeping the ice block in place. Suddenly, the crew felt the surfboard start to slide backward toward the edge of the cliff.

"Oh." Otis's voice was suddenly weak with fear.

"Ah, Otis?" Peck said weakly.

"What? What happened?" asked a frantic Freddy as the surfboard slid out over the edge.

"You know, it's times like this when I like to say OH CA-CA!" Pip yelled.

At that, the surfboard tipped over the edge of the cliff and zoomed straight down the hill at top speed.

"You didn't just do thaaaaaaaaat!" yelled Otis as they flew through the air. "AHHHHHHHHHHH!" they cried in unison. They zoomed around trees, over rocks, between water towers, and even sailed through spurting fountains of oil!

Just when they thought the worst was over, Otis realized they were in even bigger trouble. "CHICKEN FARM!" he screamed as the board careened straight into the ground, chicken feathers sticking to their already oil-covered bodies. Just a regular day on the barnyard for Otis and the crew.

Two

Hens clucked. Sheep bleated. Pigs snorted. It was time for the morning meeting. "Good morning, everyone," Ben began. The noise settled down. Ben studied the notes on his clipboard. "Okay, before we get started, we have a birthday. Everett the dog turned thirteen today."

The crowd cheered and clapped politely. A thin dog with patchy, gray fur, wearing an old birthday hat, attempted to stand up slowly. He finally raised his cane and waved to the crowd as his false teeth fell out.

"Boy, those dog years are rough, huh?" Ben added. "Also remember that it's—"

Ben didn't finish his sentence. The barn door opened as Otis and crew slid in on their surfboard, laughing and covered in chicken feathers from their run-in with the chicken farm.

Ben cleared his throat and glared at Otis.

"'Sup," Otis greeted everyone. "Oh. Ah, hey, Pop. Look, I know you're probably looking for an explanation regarding the, ah . . . exploded chicken on me, and the sticky black oil stuff," he stammered, kicking the surfboard out the barn door with his back hoof. "Ha, ha, ha, you are going to love this! I'll tell ya, because you, my friend, are a laugher—"

"Just take a seat," Ben interrupted with a sigh.

"I'll, uh, take a seat," Otis replied.

Otis slid into an empty space, passing a row of chickens. "Excuse me . . . sorry about that . . . little tight . . . okay." His buddies squeezed in next to him.

Ben cleared his throat. "As I was saying . . ."

Peck elbowed Freddy and pointed at Pig. Freddy looked and bit his tail to keep from laughing out loud.

"Hey, Pig," Peck whispered. "I think there's a dead bee in your nostril."

"Oh!" Pig replied. He twitched his nose, scrunched

his face, blocked one nostril, and blew hard. The bee popped out and hit the ground. "Well, that's not dead."

"Okay, the first matter at hand, gray-market goods. As if I needed to say it again, the purchase of human articles from the gopher underground is strictly prohibited."

Just then a cell phone's muffled techno ring echoed throughout the barn. All the animals turned toward the noise. Otis flushed red with embarrassment. He gave a wilting wave, pulled out the offending cell phone, and flipped it open.

"Hey, Otis," a gopher said from the other end of the line. He sat inside his large hole, crates of different sizes and shapes surrounding him. Behind him two gophers in coveralls were carrying a lamp. "Yeah, listen, I think your new sneakers are in. Remind me, were they the, uh, deluxe runners or the glow-in-the-dark cross trainers?"

"This really isn't the best time to talk," Otis whispered, smiling nervously at the crowd. "Ah, yeah, I really have to, uh, *run* now." Otis flipped the phone closed. "Wrong number," he said.

"Second item," Ben said. "As a reminder to everyone, standing on two legs is only permitted when humans are nowhere in sight. No close calls! You've been given a sixth sense—use it."

Otis yawned. He'd heard it all before. In the morning meetings and out of them. No watching television through the farmhouse window. No swimming in the pond. It's for drinking only. No teasing the mailman. Blah-blah-blah-blah-blah. His dad's morning speeches were as predictable as Pig getting things stuck inside his nose, but less entertaining. Otis scanned the room looking for anything to relieve the barnyard boredom.

A fly buzzed around his head. *Much* more interesting. The fly landed on Otis's ear. Otis wiggled, trying to get the fly off. The fly gave up and buzzed away. Otis's eyes followed the fly as it buzzed around the barn—a loop-de-loop, a zig-zag and a . . . ACHHEM. Ben cleared his throat, zapping Otis back to reality.

"And most important of all, let me remind you that this is coyote season."

Gasps and murmurs raced through the barn. Coyotes were their worst enemy. Even with the fence to protect them, and Ben as their guardian, the animals couldn't be too careful. Coyotes were vicious. They were cruel. And if that wasn't bad enough, they had terrible hygiene.

"They are ruthless and desperate creatures," Ben said. "Rule number one: Stay in groups. Rule number two: Stay inside the perimeter fence at all times. And rule number three: Be careful out there. Okay, let's hit it. Mooove!"

The meeting adjourned, and the animals erupted from the barn, eager to start the day. Otis leaped from his seat. He pushed his way through the stampede of animals. "And leaving quickly, walk it out, walk it out, step step, wider and . . ."

"Otis? Why don't you stick around for a minute?" Otis could tell by his father's tone, it was not a suggestion. He froze.

"He scares me, bye," Pip squeaked, hopping off Otis's shoulder and scooting from the barn. Time to turn on the old Otis charm. He turned toward his dad, flashing a big, wide bovine grin. "Dad!"

Ben kicked down a bale of hay. "Sit."

"And I'm sitting," Otis announced.

"Okay, first off, I don't even want to know who was on the other end of that phone call," Ben started. Though he really did want to know. "It *was* the gophers, wasn't it? Nope, I don't want to know." Ben paused. "Was it the gophers?" he repeated. "Nope. Don't. I don't want to know. Why do you do this to me, Otis? How do you think that makes me look?"

Otis thought for a second. "So this . . . this is about you?"

Ben sighed. "Where *were* you this morning, Otis?"

"I was having a little fun," Otis replied. "I mean, you should try it sometime. It starts with a smile, then slowly builds and—"

Ben interrupted. "You promised to help me with the brush around the fence. You know it's coyote season and—"

"Ah, jeez, Dad," Otis complained. "I don't get it. What's the big deal? They're coyotes. Them tiny, us big. What are they gonna do?"

Ben shook his head. "You have a lot to learn."

"And you know what?" Otis added. "I don't get the fence thing. It can't keep them out."

"That fence defines our space," Ben explained. "And as long as I'm still kickin', no animal will be harmed inside that fence."

"That's what you do," Otis said. "*You*. Okay? If you're trying to groom me to be the big leader, just give it up. It's not me, Pop. I mean, if I *was* in charge, things would be different. Every animal for himself, that's the way it should be."

"Otis." Ben sighed. "A strong man stands up for himself. A stronger man stands up for others."

Otis patted himself as if looking for something. "Shoot, you know what? I forgot my pen. . . ."

Ben ignored him. "And your shift tonight?"

"I'll be there."

"Otis, you're going to have to grow up one day," Ben continued. "You'll never be happy if you spend all your time goofing off."

"No? Just watch me."

Otis bopped out of the barn. Ben shook his head. *Someday*, he thought. *Someday Otis will learn.*

Three

Otis went straight to the farmer's garage and revved up the tractor.

The machine burst from the garage and roared into the open field.

Otis looked at Peck and Freddy, who were being pulled by the tractor from fluffy parachutes, parasailing in the clear blue sky.

"Hey, Freddy, is this great or what?" Peck cried with excitement.

"Yeah," Freddy said, feeling himself drifting into

another delicious fantasy about his good friend Peck. "I could just eat your head right off!" he admitted before he could control himself.

"I mean, um, you know, it's fun up here!" Freddy covered up nervously.

After lunch Otis watched a golf cart whiz past the green at the Izzy Springs Golf Course across the way. The driver didn't notice the solitary cow, grazing in the rough. When the cart was out of sight, Otis stood up and eyeballed the distance to the next hole. Pip inspected a golf ball at Otis's feet and looked at the flag thirty feet away.

"Pip?" Otis queried.

"I'd go with wood on this one," Pip suggested as he set the ball down on the golf tee.

Otis snapped a branch from a nearby oak tree. He hunkered over the ball and wiggled his butt. He wound into a mighty back swing, his nostrils flaring and his flat tongue hanging out the side of his mouth. The ball sailed through the air and dropped onto the green. Otis matched the ball's roll with contorted body language. He twisted and arched his back, scooted his arms, tapped his feet, and scrunched his face, trying to guide his ball to the eighteenth hole. It rolled and stopped a few feet from the hole.

Pip chuckled.

Otis glared at the ball. He stomped his hoof twice on the grass, hard, like thunder. The vibration bounced Pip around like a piece of popcorn with each stomp.

A gopher popped his head out from the eighteenth hole. Otis pointed to the golf ball. The gopher flashed the *okay* sign to Otis and slid back inside the ground. Seconds later the earth underneath the ball opened up. The ball sank into it. It was a hole in one. A very large hole-in-one.

"Oh, that's what I'm talking about!" Otis celebrated. "Sweet mama!"

That night the farmer finished his chores and retired to the living room. He plopped down into his favorite chair and turned on the television to watch the football game.

"Oh, man, this is sweet," Otis exclaimed.

Otis, Pip, Pig, Freddy, and Peck were peeking in through the living-room window, also enjoying the game.

"He's got the ball on the thirty," the announcer roared from the television. "He's down to the twenty, to the ten . . . looks like it's a touchdown!"

"Yahhhooo!" Otis and his friends cheered and pounded the windowsill.

"He's in!" Pig yelled.

"There you go!" Otis bellowed. "That's my man!"

They stopped suddenly and looked at one another. They'd made too much noise. They ducked from the window just as the farmer turned around. He stared at the window and blinked several times.

The farmer sighed and returned to his football game.

Four

The next day . . .

"Slurppp!" Pig chewed on a piece of corn as he sat beside Otis. Pip jumped off of Otis's shoulder and bounced on Pig's round belly. "Bacon," he said. He jumped to Otis's stomach. "Hamburger." He bounced again on Pig's belly and back to Otis's stomach. "Whoo whoo!" he yelled. "Chorizo . . . filet! Bacon . . . hamburger . . . chorizo . . . filet . . . chorizo—"

"What are you doing?" Otis asked his tiny friend.

"I'm naming the kinds of cuts of meat to the animal

I'm jumping on. Machaka. Rump roast. Pork chops."

"You know what? You don't need to be doing this," Otis reprimanded. Just then, Otis heard melodic peeps and chirps, echoing across the barnyard. It was the gentle singing of Etta's baby chicks's choir. Otis peeked between the slats of the fence. The chicks were lined up, singing their hearts out, trying hard to stay in line.

"Oaty! Oaty! Oaty! Oaty!" Otis knew the excited, high-pitched voice. Maddy, the sweetest and cutest little chick in the history of sweet and cute little chicks, was running toward Otis, her little wings flapping like a hummingbird's. "Hi, Oaty."

"Hey, Maddy. Lookin' good over there," Otis said. He reached out between the slats and picked her up.

"Chubba Face, you crazy cow!" Maddy giggled. She pushed Otis's cheeks together. "Say, 'I am smooshy'!" Maddy demanded.

"I am smooshy." Otis laughed, speaking through his pinched lips. "Okay now you. Say, 'Boy is it windy,'" Otis said, stretching Maddy's cheeks out as far as they would go.

"Boy is it windy!" Maddy repeated through a stretched mouth.

Just then, he looked through the fence and saw a new cow . . . a *beautiful* new cow, walking with a friend. She was watching him and smiling. Otis returned Maddy to the ground.

"Okay, chick," he said. "Run along now." Otis stood up and banged his head on the fence rail and plopped back to the ground. "All righty!" he said, rubbing his head.

The pretty cow laughed, but kept walking. Pip leaped onto Otis's head. "Hey," Otis asked, "who is she?"

"They just showed up. Farmer took them in," Pip responded.

"Thank you, Farmer!" Otis sang happily.

"Yeah, something happened with their herd. They're the only two that made it."

"Hmm," said Otis, deep in thought. "She could use a friend."

Otis took off after the two cows and finally caught up with them.

"Excuse me," Otis interrupted. "But I, ah, couldn't help but notice over there that . . ."

The new cow turned to face Otis. Her belly protruded from her otherwise tiny frame.

"Whoa!" Otis pointed at her stomach. "Look at you. You're all uh . . ."

"Pregnant?" she said helpfully.

"Yeah, sure, I mean, really?" Otis struggled for words. "'Cause it . . . it isn't that noticeable. Especially when you stand up straight and you don't look at it. When you turn to the side it gets a little lumpy. I mean glow-y. It's a glow . . ."

Otis's stammering brought a smile to her face. Her friend just rolled her eyes.

Otis gave up and cleared his throat. "I'm Otis."

"I'm Daisy," she replied. They shook hooves as Otis stared deeply into Daisy's eyes.

"Uh uh. Back off, Daisy." Daisy's friend pushed herself between the couple. "There's a *L* for 'loser' on this boy's forehead."

Pip climbed atop Otis's head and twisted his body to the shape of an *L*. "No, that's just me," he insisted. "Pip, the little contortion mouse!"

"*C!*" Otis yelled

Pip twisted his body, arched his back, and stuck out his arms until he resembled the letter. Otis smiled and didn't stop. He called out other letters: "*X! N! Q!*"

Pip gamely tried to contort his body to the shape of the letters. "You're killing me, dude." Pip gasped and collapsed onto Otis's snout.

"I just wanted to welcome you to the barnyard," Otis said, grinning. "I'm sure that you and your . . ."

"Oh, I came here alone," Daisy offered. "And I'm not really looking."

"Not looking," Daisy's friend repeated. "Key word: 'not.' Work with me here: She's not looking."

"This is my friend, Bessy," Daisy explained.

"Yeah, she's sweet," Otis said, smiling at Bessy.

Bessy pulled Daisy away.

"It was nice to meet you, Otis," Daisy said over her shoulder as Bessy pulled her toward the pasture. At least Otis knew her name now, and she knew his.

"Yeah, too you, ah . . . ," Otis stammered. "Uh, you know what . . . switch those. Ah boy," he mumbled to himself.

"Forget it, Otis," Pip said. "There's nothing for you there, but I kinda like her friend. *Ay, ay, ay!*"

Five

Darkness fell upon the barnyard, blanketing it with warm night air. Pip stood on Otis's head, peeking over the wooden fence. He stared at the farmhouse. A single light burned from the window. After a few seconds the light flicked off. The farmer was going to bed.

"He's out," Pip called out from his watch post.

Otis turned to the barn and let loose with a loud "Mooo!"

Inside the barn Pig was waiting on the balcony. He heard Otis's call. "All clear!" Pig cried.

"Suuuuuweeeeeeeet!" He yanked on the end of a thick rope. A panel in the roof slid open. Moonlight poured into the barn.

Two roosters tipped a metal basin on its side and caught the moonlight, reflecting the beam into a spotlight, which spattered onto a makeshift stage. Beneath the spotlight, a horse ripped into a jamming country tune, which rocked through the barn. Drumbeats rattled the barn's wooden frame, guitars squealed out the background rhythm. Everett, the aging dog, joined in, strumming his banjo, just as his false teeth fell out.

Inside the barn the animals worked quickly and in time to the music. Freddy lassoed string lights around the rafters and plugged them in, bathing the barn with a dance-hall glow. Crates were flipped over to make chairs and tables. Stalls were converted into dining booths. An old rowboat became a rustic pool table. Fresh hay covered the ground. Feed buckets were arranged in the corners.

Hog, the bartender, set up a makeshift bar along the back wall and filled several mugs with frosty cold milk. A beehive behind him dripped with fresh honey. Hog swigged some Grade "A" unpasteurized milk and placed a tip jar on the counter.

It had taken less than a minute, but the barn was now the hottest nightclub in three counties. A bull lifted the barn door's latch with his horns and kicked them open. The waiting crowd rushed in—hens, roosters, pigs, sheep, goats, horses. The whole barnyard had come to party! The hoedown was in full swing when Daisy and Bessy entered the barn. Daisy couldn't believe her eyes. "Wow, this is amazing!"

Bessy yanked two stools from underneath two big bulls at the bar. The bulls plopped to the ground, glaring at Bessy. "Hey!" the bigger one yelled to the cow.

"What are you looking at?" Bessy challenged. She puffed out her chest and stiffened her stubby legs to the ground, bracing for trouble. "You want some of this?" The bulls backed away, moving down the bar. "Didn't think so." Bessy slid the stools to a table where Daisy stood. "Sit right here, honey."

Daisy sat and sniffed the flowers on the table. "I love wild flowers." Daisy plucked one from the vase and took a bite, swallowing the petals in one gulp.

Ben didn't have time for the hoedown. He surveyed the barnyard from fence to fence, checking for signs of trouble. He had an obligation to the other animals, to ensure everyone's safety by keeping the coyotes out. Ben heard heavy footsteps, stomping through the grass. The sound was too loud for coyotes. There's only one animal those steps could belong to.

"See, Dad?" Otis exclaimed. "Right on time just like I—ooops!" Otis's hoof got caught under a bush, and he smashed face-first into the damp grass. "Cramp!" he yelped, clutching his leg. "It's cramping . . . oohhh! Oh! And release! Whew!" He let go of his leg, and it relaxed back to the ground.

"Hello, son."

Otis wobbled to his feet. He rubbed the back of his leg and brushed twigs and dirt from his hide. "Dad, I've been thinking, and, well, I'm willing to accept your apology."

"Really." Ben smiled.

"Sure," Otis replied. "It's only right. I mean . . . I don't mean to let you down, Pop. I'm just out trying to have some fun."

Ben stared at the stars in the night sky. "It's a beautiful night," he finally said. "I remember when I used to sit out here with your sister."

"I don't have a sister."

"Oh yeah," Ben replied. "That was *you*, wasn't it?"

Otis laughed and gently butted a shoulder against his father. They laughed together.

"So, are we okay?" Otis asked.

"We're okay," said Ben.

"Great. 'Cause I wanted to ask you something." Otis squirmed nervously in the grass, trying to get comfortable. "My friends are all going to the barn tonight, not that it matters either way to me, but evidently I'm needed—you know, sort of an integral part of a musical number. I tried to tell them no, you know, but they wouldn't listen. I told them, 'My dad's not going to want to cover my shift, I mean, it's my shift, not his, you know. I don't want to be selfish. What's mine is mine' and . . . you know how it is." Otis turned and faced his father. Ben's face betrayed no emotion. "So, what do you think?" Otis concluded anxiously.

Ben had heard this speech before. Otis was always trying to get out of his chores. He always seemed to have some excuse or some place to be other than where he was *supposed* to be. Ben took a deep breath. "Otis, I never thought I was going to amount to much. And I certainly didn't think I'd ever be in charge of anything. But that all changed one day. It was the day you showed up."

Otis's ears perked up.

"I was out in the meadow." Ben stopped for a moment as the memory brought a smile to his face. "And I saw this little baby calf, all alone, stumbling around. You know, before you became a nightmare. Well, I took you home that night. Well, I know it doesn't sound possible, but I looked up into the sky and I would have swore I saw the stars dance. I don't know how to explain it, but at that moment everything seemed clear to me. I knew my place was here, taking care of things. I guess you helped me realize that. I love you, son."

Ben smiled at Otis. He loved moments like this with his son. They didn't happen often, but when they did, they somehow made Ben's other problems feel so much smaller. Otis smiled back at his father.

"You still want to go, don't you?" Ben asked.

"I really do!" Otis gushed, standing up with excitement. "Not that the stuff you're saying isn't nifty and everything. It's nifty—"

"No one says 'nifty,'" Ben pointed out.

"I say 'nifty,'" Otis defended. "I do. And sometimes even 'swifty,' I'll say that."

"Oh, very impressive." Ben sighed. "Go ahead. Have fun at the hoedown. I'll cover your shift."

"Thanks, Pop!" Otis enthused. "You're the best!"

Otis jumped up from the grass, feeling lighter than air, and turned toward the barn.

"Otis, be the stronger man," Ben called to his son.

"Yeah, yeah, that's that saying thing. A strong man stands up for himself," Otis replied. "A stronger man can bridge the gap between . . . yeah, uh, got it! Locked in the vault!" Otis managed a clean leap over the bush this time. No tripping, falling, or face planting. "See! I learned."

Otis galloped through the meadow, down toward the barn without a care in the world. Ben smiled and shook his head. *Someday*, he thought.

Off in the distance, a coyote's howl broke the peaceful night air. Ben's eyes narrowed and focused. He resumed his watch.

Six

"Who's here! Moo! It's me—moo! What's up? AHH, milk me!" Otis exclaimed, bursting into the barn. "My barn. That's right! My barn."

Otis spotted Daisy. He smiled and, in his daze, slammed into a waiter. A tray flew into the air, and Otis and the waiter crashed to the ground. Dishes clattered around them. Milk splashed onto the floor.

"He's a real winner, that one," Bessy said, motioning toward Otis.

"Oh, stop it," Daisy replied. "I think he's kind of cute."

On stage, Biggie Cheese, a chubby mouse, was finishing up his rap song. The emcee, Root, jumped to the stage as Biggie took his final bow and blew a kiss to the audience. "How about a *biggie* hand for Biggie Cheese!" Root yelled to the crowd.

The audience roared their approval as the heavy mouse waddled off the stage. "Now, tonight we're going to have some fun, y'all." Root prowled the stage like a tiger ready to pounce. He saw a horse resting his feet on the stage. "Hey, buck, get your hooves off the stage. You ain't in show business!"

The audience laughed as the horse sheepishly put his feet back on the floor. "Were you raised in a barn?" Root continued. He looked out over the audience. "What are you looking at, Turkey?"

There was a table full of turkeys seated in the far corner. They giggled at being singled out.

"Hey, somebody pass me the cranberry sauce!" Root screamed. The audience laughed. The turkeys looked around the barn, worried they might spot a hidden tub of mashed potatoes and gravy to seal their doom. "Dead turkey walkin'!" Root continued. "We're all gonna die, but we don't know the date. We know *your* date—Thanksgiving!" Root laughed, and the audience joined in the fun. Pigs oinked and snorted.

Horses whinnied. Dogs howled with delight.

"Okay, to kick things off tonight, I got a special treat for us," Root said. "Back by popular demand, ladies, this one's for you—our own Otis and the Crew!"

Two mice hopped on the piano keys, tinkling out a musical introduction. The spotlight shined on Otis. He put his hat and dark sunglasses on, and hopped onto the banister. He slid down and landed on the stage, greeted by the explosive screams and whistles of the eager audience.

"Oh, milk me!" Otis cried out in response. He pointed to his friends and gave Daisy a big grin, momentarily lowering his sunglasses to look her in the eyes.

She returned his smile.

Otis was in the spotlight, and he couldn't have been happier. Pig, Pip, Peck, and Freddy danced behind him. Otis sang his heart out. He strutted across the stage like he owned it. Sweat poured from his leather hide like milk from a bottle. Otis boogied closer and closer to the edge of the stage until he jumped off. He finished his song on his knees and tossed his hat to Daisy.

"Moo!" he cried to a standing ovation from the crowd.

Outside, across the field, Mrs. Beady had her nosy eye on the farmer's barn. She peeked out her living-room window, glaring. She saw the flashing lights, heard the squeals and whistles of the audience, and felt the dance music thumping through the darkness.

"Parties all hours of the night," she complained. "What is that farmer up to? What does he do over there all night? I'm going to call someone!"

While his wife stared out the window, Mr. Beady watched television. "Leave him be," he insisted.

Mrs. Beady huffed and dropped into her chair. She picked up her knitting and clacked the needles together. Under her breath she mumbled, "Well, I'll just call whoever I want and whenever I want to, that's exactly what I'll do. Because I know what a rave is. Mr. Lumpy's gonna sit and watch his TV and be a lump." She glared at her husband. "Well, okay, Mr. Lumpy? It's just not right."

But Mr. Beady wasn't listening. His reply was a deep, peaceful snore. "Harrumph!" Mrs. Beady grumbled. Her needles clacked together with greater ferocity, then suddenly stopped as quickly as they had begun.

Mrs. Beady stared at the telephone on the table next to her. This noise was just unacceptable, and she was going to do something about it.

Seven

In the distance, a car with flashing red lights and sirens wailing drove down the path that led to the barn. After three loud hoots, an owl finally managed to signal the animals, and the barn went silent. Suddenly, there was a knock at the barn door. Shock filled the barn.

"I'll check it," said Pip, jumping up on the windowsill to peer down. Pip rubbed the fog from the window and realized the car with flashing red lights was *not* a cop car; it was the delivery car from Siren Pizza. "It's all right, calm down. It's just the pizza guy."

A sigh of relief came over the crowd.

"I'm on it!" yelled Otis, running over to the door. He and Pig got into position to deal with the pizza boy. Pig climbed on top of Otis, a mannequin's plastic arm in his hand. Otis held another, and together they stuck the arms out the barn door to accept the delivery with a wad of cash in their fake human hands.

"Whoa, uh, thanks. You need change?" the oblivious pizza boy asked.

"No, keep it," Otis said nervously.

"So, you really ordered a lot of pizzas," the delivery boy remarked, passing ten or so pies into the extended plastic arms.

"Well, yes," Otis stammered. "We're having a big human party, just a party to celebrate our human-ness," Otis finally finished.

"Dude, I love parties!" the pizza boy exclaimed. "Can I come?"

"No," Otis barked immediately, almost causing Pig to topple off his shoulders.

"Okay, then, well, I'll see ya," the boy remarked, dejected. Suddenly, Pig couldn't hold the position any longer and lost his grip on the plastic arm. It fell out the barn doors, onto the ground where the pizza boy was standing. The boy let out a scream.

"Ouch!" Otis remarked, attempting to keep up the facade. "My arm fell off. Ah, my ah, fake arm, I mean."

"Wow. I am so sorry about that. Do you need any help?" the boy asked.

"No, I don't like help," Otis responded quickly. "Uh, it's just against my religion. I'm a No-helpian."

"Oh, cool. I'm a Lutheran. What about this?" he asked.

"You know what, you keep it. Yeah. It's dirty now."

"Really? All right." Then he turned away from the barn and headed back toward his car. "Dude," he yelled to his twin brother. "I got an arm!"

Eight

It was after midnight when Ben picked up his guitar and gently plucked the strings. Thunder boomed across the sky. Lightning flickered in the distance. A storm was coming, but the soft notes of Ben's guitar reassured any who could hear that their protector was on duty.

Across the barnyard a band of coyotes snuck through the grass, like commandos on a secret mission. The thunder crashed, and the coyotes crawled under the fence, one at a time. Their paws made no sound on the damp meadow. Low to the ground and out of sight, they eased past Ben's watchful gaze toward their target: the henhouse.

Dag, the leader of the vicious pack, emerged first from the meadow and slithered across the barnyard. His matted fur hugged his lean, scraggly frame, and his sharp teeth glinted in the moonlight. Dag reached the henhouse and pushed open the wooden door. The hens were fast asleep. Dag thrust out his claw and wrapped it around the throat of the first chicken he saw. She struggled desperately for air, but only a strangled cry sputtered out. It was just enough to wake the others.

"Good evening, ladies," Dag said to the awakening hens, snarling. "Sorry to call on you so late in the evening, but we had a previous engagement." Dag held out a metal key ring. Several pairs of chicken feet were dangling from it like trophies. The hens gasped in horror.

"We're only going to take six of you tonight," Dag reassured. "Anyone who makes a sound can join us too. We don't mind the extra company."

Dag snapped his fingers. His pack entered the henhouse on cue, sizing up the terrified hens.

"You won't be taking any hens tonight," Etta stated boldly to Dag.

The powerful coyote turned to Etta and growled. He leaned his face close to hers. His sharp teeth were dripping with saliva. His breath was hot and moist. Dag grinned. "And you're going to stop us, hen? Is that what's gonna happen? How are you going to do that?"

"No," Etta said, pointing to the door, "he is."

Dag turned. A silhouette stood in the doorway. Lightning crackled, casting a flashing white glow across Ben's angry face. Dag played it cool.

"Ben! How are you, Ben? I would have said hello had we seen you."

"Put the hen down, Dag," Ben ordered.

"Sure, Ben, whatever you say. We're just doing a little courtin,' that's all. You know how much we like the hens." Dag laughed as he set his victim back down into her nest. "You know me. Lady-killer." Dag glanced around at the rest of his pack. "You have us at a bit of a disadvantage here, Ben. There's six of us and only one old, fat you."

Dag nodded to his pack. The coyotes moved slowly toward Ben, stalking him, circling him. Ben stood at the ready, his guitar with him. He counted the coyotes and took careful note as to where each coyote was. One of them moved closer to Ben on his right side. The coyote leaped at Ben.

Wham!

Ben swung his guitar down on the attacking coyote, smacking the predator's head with an out-of-tune *twang*. The coyote fell backward, and his friends growled and moved closer, jumping at Ben, clawing at him, trying to sink their teeth into his hide.

Ben swung his guitar like a ninja warrior, swatting the coyotes as fast as they came at him. He turned to his left. *Swat!* He turned to his right. *Bap!* As his pack was thumped one by one, Dag backed away into the shadows, circling Ben.

As soon as Ben's back was turned, Dag pounced. He sliced through the air and slammed into Ben. The surprise attack pushed Ben out of the henhouse door and into the muddy barnyard. Rain poured from the dark sky. The big cow stumbled and fell to the ground. He felt the coyotes' claws and fangs dig into him. The pain was intense, but Ben would not give up. He threw out his hoof and punched one coyote, then swatted another with his guitar. Coyote after coyote sailed through the air as Ben returned to his feet.

At that moment Dag lowered his head, bared his fangs in a vicious grimace, and leaped for Ben's leg. The coyote's razor-sharp teeth dug into Ben's flesh. Ben howled in anguish and fell over. His face twisted with pain. The pack angrily mobbed him as Dag turned toward the henhouse. Ben thrust his right hoof from the pack and grabbed Dag's hind leg. Dag yelped in shock. Ben stood up, pulling Dag up along with him.

Ben ignored his injured leg and swung Dag like a club, knocking the other coyotes away. They backed off, warily circling Ben. Ben slammed Dag into a tree and gripped his throat. Dag's eyes widened with fear. He was scared. Ben raised his free hoof and folded it into a tight fist.

Ben could have ended Dag's threat once and for all. But he didn't. He wasn't going to stoop down to Dag's level—he was going to be the better man. So he let Dag go, and the coyote fell to the ground. He coughed and gasped for breath, then retreated into the rainy night. His pack followed him out of the barnyard, howling after their leader, humiliated and defeated.

Ben had won. No hens were taken. The barnyard was safe. As soon as the coyotes were out of sight, Ben dropped to his knees with a strangled cry. He collapsed to the ground.

"Ben!" Etta gasped. She ran from the henhouse to the barn. She could hear music blaring nonstop, mixed with the shuffle of dancing feet and the cackle of party animals having a good time. She flapped into an open window, frantic.

47

"Otis! Otis!" Etta screamed. She ran through the crowd, dodging their legs and ankles. "Otis!"

Otis stared at the shaken Etta. "It's Ben!" she cried out. Otis saw the look on Etta's face. He didn't need to hear another word.

Otis burst from the barn and ran toward the henhouse, galloping on all fours. Ben lay in the grass on the hill, motionless. Several hens paced quietly around him.

Otis dropped to the ground next to his father and cradled his head. "Oh no. No, no, no . . ." Otis wept. Ben opened his eyes and stared at his son for a moment. He touched Otis lovingly on the shoulder. A look of peace rose in Ben's face. He closed his eyes one final time.

Ben was gone.

Nine

The next morning the farmer stood at the edge of his cornfield. He dumped the last shovelful of dirt onto Ben's grave and gently patted it with his hand. "Good cow," he said sadly, and walked to the farmhouse.

When he was out of sight, Pip, Freddy, Pig, Peck, Miles, and the other animals slowly approached Ben's grave. Their heads were low with sadness. Tears filled their eyes. Daisy gave Etta a bouquet of wildflowers to place on the grave. She asked if anyone had seen Otis. No one had seen him for hours.

Otis sat in the grass at the last place he'd been with his father, on top of the hill near the fence. Memories of Ben flooded through his brain. He stared across the creek and thought of the time his father taught him how to fish in that water. He remembered the feel of the fishing pole in his little hooves.

All right, now, Otis, just lift, Ben had said. *It's like the hands of a clock. Ten and two. Ten and two.* Little Otis had thrown the line toward the water and had whacked his father in the head. Not once. Not twice. But many, many times.

Not like that, Ben had said patiently. *Now lift toward two o'clock and . . . ow . . . ow.* Eventually Ben had been tangled in little Otis's fishing line and had fallen into the water, and the two had just laughed and laughed. His father had jokingly called him "fisherman." It was just one of many great days together.

Otis smiled briefly before the sadness overwhelmed him again.

Ten

"What do we do now?" one animal asked.

Inside the barn a meeting was in progress. With Ben gone, there were questions that needed answers.

"Who's going to protect us from the coyotes?"

"Order!" Duke stood front and center. "Order here! Let's get this meeting started." He glared at the crowd.

Peck raised a feathered wing. "Hey, Duke, who's going to run the meeting?"

"That's what the meeting's about," Duke answered.

"So the meeting's about finding someone to run the meeting?" Freddy queried. "Is that a good idea?"

"We should have a meeting about it," Pip suggested.

"Someone has to do this, we don't have Ben," Duke stated. "Therefore I would like to nominate myself."

The animals snickered and giggled at Duke's suggestion. Pig shook his head. Pip laughed.

Duke puffed out his chest. "Listen to me. Dogs are watchful, they're loyal and very protective."

"You chase your own tail," Pip said, laughing.

"I don't do that," Duke shouted indignantly, then added, "anymore. One time when I was bored I chased it . . . just a little bit . . . around the room . . ."

"Yeah, and I saw you drink out of the toilet once," Pig called out. "Hey, you drink potty water!"

"You drink potty water," the crowd sang. "You drink potty water!" The meeting was out of control now.

"My bowl was empty, my friend!" Duke sputtered, trying to restore order. "Come on, we're getting off track here!"

"Duke," interjected Miles, "with all respect, I think there are certain traits that make you unqualified to be leader."

"Yeah, such as?" Duke asked.

Without saying a word, Miles tossed a blue ball across the barn, knowing Duke couldn't resist running after it. Miles was right.

"Your point?" Duke asked, dropping the saliva-soaked ball from his mouth. "Hey, I do that for fun, not 'cause I have to, come on."

So Miles threw the ball again. Duke stood there, pretending he didn't care and trying so hard to act cool. But the excitement got the better of him, and again Duke couldn't resist. A weak expression spread across his face, and he jetted after the ball.

"So big deal, I fetch balls. One little flaw," Duke pleaded. "All right, all right, let's take a vote. All those in favor of me being our new leader?"

Duke scanned the crowd. He counted the raised hands. There were three of them, all dogs. A tiny cat sat nervously next to them. One of the dogs snarled, and the cat quickly raised his paw.

"Those opposed?" Duke queried.

Every other hand went up.

"Can you see my hand?" Pip asked.

The barn erupted with laughter. Miles cleared his throat. He sauntered up to the front of the crowd. "Listen now, listen up." The crowd calmed down. The laughter stopped. "You all know that Ben always intended for Otis to take his place."

"All right!" Pig enthused. He leaped from his seat, his big belly nearly causing him to topple over. "Otis in charge! I second that motion! Suuuweeeeeett!"

"Yeah! Otis!"

All hands went up as a celebration broke out at the thought of Otis, the party boy, being in charge. It was unanimous. Otis was now the leader of the barnyard.

"Here we go," Miles said softly under his breath.

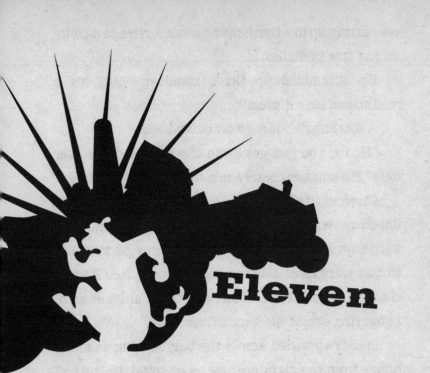

Eleven

Otis was on his way back to the barnyard with Etta and her chicks. Maddy was sitting in Otis's hoof, trying to cheer him up. But their brief moment of playfulness came to a screeching halt the moment Otis saw the barnyard. His jaw dropped open, and he stood still in a stunned silence.

"Oh, goodness gracious!" Etta exclaimed.

Chaos had broken out. A chicken came shooting out of a homemade slingshot. A cow bolted by as he was being chased by three crazy mice. A herd of sheep was sitting up in a tree helping some turtles parachute off the tree branches.

Pip scrambled up Otis's shoulder. "Oat, it's a madhouse! Isn't it great?"

A soccer ball bounced off Otis's head.

"Ha ha, you just got hit in the head with a soccer ball!" Pip laughed, barely able to control himself.

Otis looked through the open barn doors. Another hoedown was in progress—in broad daylight! The Barn Boys were jamming out their favorite party tunes. Horses were river dancing on the stage, their hooves clattering against the wood floor. Other animals were boogeying across the barn's floor.

Freddy sprawled across the bar, sucking as much honey from the giant beehive as he could. He burped loudly and went back for more.

Miles strolled over to Otis. "I thought I'd be the first to congratulate you, Otis. You're in charge now."

"I'm what?!" Suddenly the hoedown didn't matter. Otis spun to face Miles. "Whoa! Whoa! Whoa! Miles! I am *not* in charge! Okay? I don't do . . . in charge. This is not my responsibility."

"I hear you. But you were elected, fair and square." Miles walked away, leaving Otis staring after him. "Congratulations, boss."

Otis turned toward the barn and stood in the doorway. He took a deep breath. "HEY!" he screamed at the top of his lungs.

The band stopped in midsong; the horses froze in midstep. Everyone turned to Otis. The party came to an immediate halt. "Have you all lost your mind?" Otis demanded, stomping into the barn. "It's daylight! The farmer's gonna be back soon. This is sooo off-limits!"

"Come on, Otis!" Freddy teased, popping out from behind the counter. "I know your weak spot. . . ." Freddy turned to the other animals and chanted. "Wild Mike! Wild Mike! Wild Mike!"

The others joined in: "Wild Mike! Wild Mike!"

"Oh no, I'm not doing this, okay?" Otis crossed his arms and did his best to ignore their chants. "There's no way this is happening! Everybody just go back to your designated quadrants!" The animals stared blankly at him. "This is ridiculous. I'm not going to dance just because you get Wild Mike out here." He turned to Pip. "Help me out here."

"You can't fight it, Otis!" Pip yelled. "You were born a party animal!" Pip was right. He knew that Otis could never say no to a party. Or to Wild Mike.

"Wild Mike! Wild Mike! Wild Mike!" the chanting continued. Freddy pushed a wooden crate onto the stage. Small round air holes were punched in the top. A metal pin held the door latch closed. DO NOT OPEN was scrawled in big red letters on the side. The box shook and rocked. Something was inside . . . something that wanted out!

The crowd cheered. Wild Mike had arrived!

The band started to play again. The thumping beat shook the crate, rocking it back and forth on its edges. The latch shook loose and rattled to the ground. The door dropped open. A fuzz ball with feet burst from inside, its crazy fur bursting in all directions, like a giant hair ball.

Wild Mike was free!

"Wild Mike! Wild Mike! Wild Mike!" The crowd erupted into cheers. They clapped their hands together, encouraging the ragged fur ball. Wild Mike's big eyes bulged from underneath his mop of floppy hair. He danced around the crate, hopping, bouncing, shaking, and shuffling his feet. His eyes popped so wide, they almost sprang out from his hairy head.

Wild Mike's dancing energized the band. They played faster and louder. The music made Wild Mike dance even wilder. He shook his feet, his scraggly hair flying from side to side, like grass in a hurricane.

Otis felt the music pulse through his body. He

tingled with rhythm. He bounced with the bass. Otis bit his lip. He covered his ears and closed his eyes. He locked his knees and tried to ignore the music. He was determined to stand his ground.

His hips had other plans.

They twisted, bumped, and swayed to the heavy bass as if they had a mind of their own. Otis wanted to stop them. Otis *tried* to stop them, but soon the infectious motion went from his hips to his arms, and then all the way down to his feet! But the moment Wild Mike scrambled beneath Otis's legs, his willpower came crashing down, and Otis let loose with a wild flurry of dance moves!

"Let's boogie!" Otis waved his arms in the air.

Otis and Wild Mike danced side by side. Wild Mike shook his hips, and Otis shook his hips too. Wild Mike twisted on the floor, and Otis did the same. Wild Mike jumped, flipped in midair, and landed on his feet. Otis jumped. Animals rushed into the barn to join the excitement. Daisy and Bessy followed everyone in.

"Look at that freaky thing!" Bessy cried out. She tilted her head at Wild Mike. His body gyrated and spun, like the blades of a lawn mower.

"What kind of animal is that?" Daisy inquired.

"I don't know, but he sure can dance." Otis shuffled

past Daisy and Bessy. He followed Wild Mike and bumped his hips to the beat of the music. "Woo hoo haow!"

Then the music slowed. The guitars eased, and the drummer tapped out a delicate beat. The song was soft and gentle, quiet and relaxing. Wild Mike collapsed on the stage as if the air had been let out of him. Otis and the rest of the audience dropped to the ground too. They lay silent, their eyes closed. The music slowed to a whisper, so soft the crowd could barely hear it. Wild Mike didn't move. Neither did Otis. "I say let's kill it. Hand me that piece of wood over there," Bessy said.

Then the music increased in volume again. Wild Mike's right leg twitched. Otis's right leg twitched. The music grew louder. The guitars joined in. Wild Mike was shaking, like a cheerleader's pom-pom. Otis duplicated Wild Mike's every move. Slowly Wild Mike jumped to his feet. Otis and the audience followed suit, dancing and moving as if their feet were on fire.

Within seconds the barn was rocking again. Wild Mike danced in a wild blur of legs and hair. He twisted, turned, flipped, and flopped. Wherever Wild Mike went, whatever Wild Mike did, Otis followed. First one leg, then the other. Wild Mike moved faster than anything had ever moved. Then, with one big *woosh*, Wild Mike flew back into his crate. The door slammed behind him as the band hit a final crescendo.

"Wild Mike! Wild Mike! Wild Mike!" the crowd chanted. They cheered and applauded. The barn was electric.

"Whoo hoo, hoo, hoo! Whoo hoo!" Otis cheered and kept dancing. "Woo hoo! Woo hoo!" Otis spun. He twisted. He shook. Then all the animals suddenly stopped moving. A few seconds later, Otis noticed he was the only one still dancing. He turned around and faced the barn door.

Otis stopped. Cold.

The farmer stood in the doorway. He stared, agape, at Otis. Cows dancing? Chickens cheering? Horses drinking mugs of fresh milk?

Otis and his friends were caught. They had violated the prime rule of the barnyard and of Mother Nature: Stand on two legs *only* when humans are not in sight. Otis gently dropped down on all fours. There was only one thing Otis could say: "Ah . . . moo?"

WHAM! Miles knocked the farmer unconscious to the ground. He lay in the doorway, snoring soundly.

"What did you do that for?!" Otis yelled.

"What else was I gonna do?" Miles defended. "He saw you."

"You could've killed him!" Otis said.

Pip hopped on the farmer's wrist. "I got a pulse." Pip raised his hands in the air. "Wheee!"

Otis sighed in relief, then realized they had a bigger problem: *What now?* He paced the barn, thinking. "This is bad. Oh, this is sooo bad." He passed by a group of sheep.

"Baaad," the sheep repeated. "Baaad."

"Everybody just calm down, all right!" Pig yelled. He began pacing around the farmer's body. The pacing turned into racing, and he threw his hooves into the air in a panic. "What are we gonna do? What are we gonna do?"

Pip, Freddy, and Peck scanned the crowd, looking for answers to Pig's question. They looked at one another and smiled. They knew exactly what to do. They slowly turned their attention back to Otis, their newly elected leader.

Otis noticed everyone staring at him. "What?" he cried.

"Come on," Pip explained. "You're our leader. Lead us."

Otis was stunned. There was only one thing to do: Make an excuse. "That does not apply to this," he said quickly. "This is totally, situationally different."

"Okay, then we gotta ditch the body," Freddy

suggested. "He knows too much. We gotta take care of him. Whack him."

Otis didn't want everything to go crazy. "There will be no whacking, all right? The farmer's a good guy—he's been good to us."

"And he's a vegan, God bless him," Miles stated.

"And, ah, what *is* a vegan again?" Pig asked.

"Oooh! I know this one!" Peck raised his wing in the air, hoping that someone would call on him.

"Nope, I got it," Pip explained. "It means you can't eat anything with a face."

"No, no, no," Peck corrected. "*That's* a vegetarian."

"Vegetarians have to eat in the dark, right?" Pig asked, confused.

"That's a vampire," Duke said.

"They can't eat cheese?" Pip guessed.

"It's not just cheese," Bessy stated. "Vegans can't have *any* dairy products."

"Cake?" Peck asked.

"Cake has egg products," Duke answered.

"But vegans can't have *any* dairy," Pip added.

"What? No dairy?" Freddy was shocked. "I *love* dairy. Does that mean I can't be a vegan?"

"I love the smell of bacon," Pig confessed, covering his face with his hooves. "There, I said it."

The farmer groaned. He was waking up. Everyone froze. His foot twitched. He sat up on his knees, wobbly, shaking his head. He stared at the animals in his barn. They stared back.

WHAM!

Miles knocked the farmer unconscious. Again.

"Would you stop doing that?" Otis yelled.

"It's not like we have a lot of options," Miles said.

Pip ran to the farmer and admired the red knot throbbing on his forehead. "Boy, that's a doozy. That thing's bigger than me."

"Push it," Pig suggested.

Pip's tiny finger hovered over the bump. "If he wakes up, you've got my back, right?" Pip asked.

"Yeah," Pig agreed.

Otis paced the barn. Everyone watched him, waiting to hear what his big plan would be. Otis looked at Miles. The mule just shrugged.

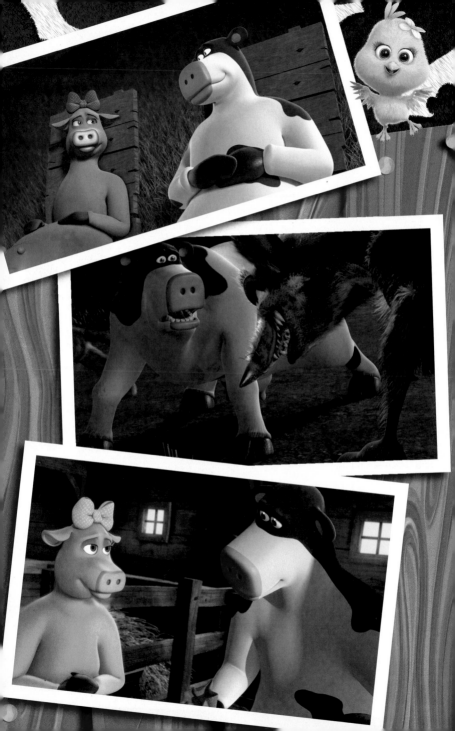

Twelve

"Come on! Come on!" Pig urged.

Otis grunted. He had come up with a plan. Otis and the other animals dragged the farmer from the barn. They placed him on the ground and leaned him up against the trunk of an old apple tree.

As the farmer slumped, Pip ran to the top of his head. "Okay, watch this," he said. "Off the nose, on the belly, on the ground. Check it."

"One, two, three!" Pip dove off the farmer's head and sprung off his soft, bulbous nose. Pip landed on

the farmer's soft stomach. His belly squished, like a trampoline, and vaulted Pip into the air. He flipped and landed on the ground. The tiny mouse wobbled for a second, caught his balance, and stuck the landing.

"Not bad, eh?" Pip took a bow.

Freddy handed Otis the farmer's hat. Otis adjusted it on the farmer's head. Pig gave Otis a book. Otis opened it and placed it on the farmer's lap.

"Okay, now," Otis explained. "He was sitting here, he was reading, and something fell on his head, and . . ."

"I got it." Pip scrambled up the apple tree and scurried down with a bright red apple. He tossed it at the farmer's head. It gently bounced off and landed on the book.

"Uh-uh, too light," Otis observed. "Couldn't cause a bump like that."

Freddy picked up the apple. "I'll bet it could." He rocked back, like a baseball pitcher, and heaved the apple. It struck the farmer's head, beaning him.

"Would you cut it out!?" Otis reprimanded. "We need something bigger."

"Ah, can I have the apple?" Pig picked it off the ground and took a bite.

Otis reached into the apple tree and gripped a heavy branch. He pulled on it, hard, until it cracked.

66

He broke the branch from the tree and set it next to the farmer. "There," Otis said. "Let's go." Otis and his friends skulked down the field to see what would happen next.

Within minutes the farmer stirred. He groaned and rubbed his head. He looked at the branch next to him and the book in his lap.

Otis and the others watched. "He's buying it," Freddy pointed out. The farmer glanced toward the barn. "He's not buying it." Freddy changed his mind. "He's buying it. Nope, he's not buying it. . . ."

Otis clamped his hoof over Freddy's mouth. He stared intently at the farmer. "No. He's buying it." But then a shock wave shot through Otis's bovine body. The farmer was missing his right shoe! They must have left it back at the barn.

The farmer stared at his shoeless foot, then looked toward the barn. The farmer stood up and began walking across the barnyard.

WHAM!

Miles knocked the farmer to the ground. Unconscious. *Again.*

Otis ran to the barn, arms waving frantically. "Will you stop doing that!"

"Well, unless you get him a blindfold," Miles replied,

shrugging his shoulder, "I'm gonna kick him."

"Okay, let's go," Otis sighed.

They dragged the farmer back to the apple tree and leaned him against the trunk . . . again. This time Otis made sure the farmer had on both of his shoes. Otis broke off a second branch and placed it next to the first one. Two shoes. Two branches. Two bumps on the farmer's head. Otis smiled. Now *this* was a plan.

They left the sleeping farmer against the tree with the book in his lap. They again retreated down the field to watch their plan in action. Moments later the farmer stirred. He opened his eyes and rubbed his head, gently touching the bumps on his forehead. He saw the book in his lap, the branches on the ground, and looked up into the tree. Dazed he stood and shuffled toward the barn.

The farmer opened the barn door and looked inside. A single chicken clucked and pecked at the ground— just like a chicken should. There was no music. No band. No dancing animals. The farmer shook his head and headed to his house. He looked back at the barn one last time, but there was nothing to see.

"See? Good as new," Otis said, pleased with himself. "This in-charge thing isn't so tough, huh?"

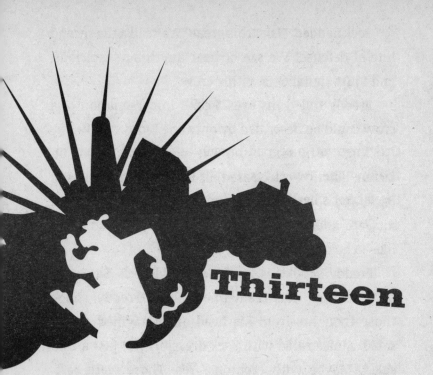

Thirteen

At sundown Otis left the chicken coop and pulled the door behind him. He knocked twice, and from inside the coop, he heard the door secured by the chickens.

Inside the chicken coop the hens sat nervously in their nests. Freddy and Peck paced the floor. Freddy stared at the chickens. There were so many tasty ones, all within easy arm's reach. "Oh, hi ya, chickens," he said to all of them, licking his lips nervously. "So, ah, this was all Otis's idea?"

Peck nodded. "Isn't this great? We're like the second line of defense! We see or hear anything suspicious, and I just signal Otis with a crow."

Freddy rolled his eyes. Peck's impersonation of a crow could be described by only one word: "awful."

"Oh," Peck said, "and I've been working on it. Listen, listen." Peck cleared his throat, threw his head back, and opened his beak wide. He snapped his head forward and emitted a gasping wheeze that sounded like a choking pigeon.

Freddy shook his head. Same old Peck. Same old tasty, plump, and ready-to-eat Peck. Freddy shook those thoughts from his head and imagined a nice salad. A nice salad with Peck dressing. No! Just a nice salad. Maybe with croutons. Yes. Those were safe. Croutons.

"Well, you know, in the moment it'll be really strong," Peck explained. "But for now, let's just stand watch."

"Yeah." Freddy giggled nervously, surveying the plump chickens. "Stand and watch . . ." Freddy watched the chickens. He watched as they all morphed into plump roasted drumsticks, ready for tasting, ready for dinner. Freddy started drooling, his eyes wide. "I'm not hungry. I'm not hungry. . . ."

"Freddy, are you okay?" Peck stepped into a puddle of drool on the ground.

"Boneless white meat!" Freddy blurted out in reply. "Drumsticks!"

Peck looked at his friend, confused. "Freddy!"

"What?" Freddy asked. He quickly shifted his eyes to the ground. "I'm not hungry. I mean, I don't want to eat anyone, thing, I mean, you."

Fourteen

Otis made his way around the perimeter of the barnyard, making sure all was in order.

"Okay, a little once-around-the-barnyard, then hellooo party-y!"

That's when he spotted a few kids sneaking up on a sleeping cow on top of the hill.

"Hey, hey, hey," came a voice from behind. "Look at this, it's our new inside connection."

"Congratulations, Otis!" The yell interrupted Otis's thoughts. He looked up and saw Eddy, Igg, and Bud,

the Jersey cows. Ben had never liked the Jerseys, but Otis knew they were always ready for a good time. They were fun cows. Contented cows. Despite their body brandings and ear tags, Otis always got along with them.

Eddy pointed down the meadow. "Oh, will you look at that." He, too, had noticed the boys on the hill.

The boys had snuck through the tall grass. They crept up to a sleeping cow. "Shhh . . . this is awesome!" Willy, the leader of the group, said. He placed his hands gently on the side of the cow and shoved as hard as he could. The shocked cow fell over with a *thud*! The cow let out a horrified moo. Her feet kicked wildly in the air, looking for support. The cow rocked back and forth, trying to roll over.

"That's called cow tipping! Ha ha ha!" Willy laughed. Mission accomplished, the boys ran from the field. They jumped the fence and hopped onto their bicycles.

"That so steams me!" Eddy growled; his hooves clenched with rage.

Igg was equally upset. "Man, I wish I could get a hold of that boy. . . ."

Otis glanced at the helpless cow, struggling to right herself. He watched the boys pedal down the road.

A sudden realization hit him like a bolt of lightning. "Hey, I'm in charge, right?" The Jersey cows looked at Otis and nodded.

"Oh, oh, oh, we are so talking," Eddy replied, hoping that Otis had something fun in mind. "Are we not talking here?"

"Talking the talk and walking the walk," Igg added.

"Walk-y talk-y," Bud agreed.

"Then let's go."

Otis led them through the meadow to the Beady farmhouse next door. Inside, Mrs. Beady put down her knitting and complained. "I hear music over there again. Do you hear music?" Mr. Beady didn't answer. His eyes remained glued to the television. "That farmer is out of control," she continued. "We should call someone. We should call someone!"

Mr. Beady sighed and changed the channel on the TV. Realizing her husband was not going to do anything, Mrs. Beady picked up her knitting again and angrily clacked the needles together.

Fifteen

Otis tried to keep the Jersey cows quiet as they approached the Beady's house. Eddy, Igg, and Bud kept muttering to themselves, trying to figure out what Otis was up to.

"Shhh! Shhh!" Otis cautioned. "Stop it! Be quiet!" He dropped to his belly and crawled beneath the farmhouse's window. "I'm up. I'm up."

Otis snuck along the outside of the house toward Mrs. Beady's car.

Eddy, Igg, and Bud followed Otis. Eddy went first,

then Bud. Igg crawled beneath the window, but couldn't resist a peek inside. Mrs. Beady was glaring out the window toward the music from the barn. Suddenly her eyes widened. The back of Igg's head slinked just beneath her window.

"Randall, there is a cow outside," Mrs. Beady said.

"This is a cow farm," Mr. Beady snapped. "You're gonna find cows outside."

"No, I mean right outside our house, looming, like a ghost, like a reaper!"

Mr. Beady replied, "No, cows don't like houses much. They prefer it out in the meadow, where they can get a graze on." Mr. Beady was an old-school farmer. He knew his cows.

"Nathan Randall Beady the Third, there is a cow outside!" Mrs. Beady yelled. "A large cow crawling around outside our window, trying to watch our TV!"

Mr. Beady turned up the volume. If anybody was going to watch TV right now, it would be him.

Outside, Otis snuck up the driveway to Mrs. Beady's car. He opened the driver's-side door and squeezed his massive body behind the steering wheel. The Jersey cows joined him inside the tiny car. They gently shut the doors.

"You're on my foot again," Eddy griped. "Will you get off!"

"Sorry," Bud apologized.

"This is so sweet," Eddy whispered. "So wicked sweet. I love the new you, Otis."

"Okay, Igg, you remember how to do this?" Otis queried.

"Do I!" Igg replied.

"He remembers!" Bud said.

"He's remembering," Eddy said.

"Right now," Bud added.

Igg leaned over into the driver's seat and pulled out two small wires from beneath the dashboard and twisted them together. The wires sparked, and the car started. Igg smiled with satisfaction.

Otis shifted the car into neutral, and it rolled down the driveway. It drifted over the loose gravel, crunching it underneath the tires. Otis glanced back at the Beady's farmhouse. The coast was clear.

Then he shifted into drive and stepped on the accelerator, fishtailing onto the road. The weight of the cows sank the car low to the ground. It hit a dip in the road and bottomed out. Sparks flew.

"Well, pinch me, I'm dreaming!" Eddy cried out. "Here is a first! Otis joining us on a midnight joyride. That's the animal sin of sins, ah?"

"Yeah," Bud exclaimed.

"Hey, Bud," Eddy asked. "Did you bring the good stuff?"

Bud pulled out a six-pack of white glass bottles filled with fresh milk.

"It's right here," Bud said.

"Show it," Eddy requested.

"It's right here," Bud repeated.

"Show it," Eddy demanded.

"It's. Right. Here!" Bud said. He waved the bottles in Eddy's face.

"Oh." Eddy leaned out the car window. "We're rebels! We're rebels!"

In a few minutes Otis and the Jersey cows spotted the cow-tipping boy and his friends on their bikes. The boys turned into a housing development, pedaling toward their homes.

"Too bad we can't go in there," Igg said.

"Yeah," Bud agreed.

"Breaks my heart." Eddy sighed.

"Who says we can't?" Otis smiled. He switched off the car's headlights, turned the wheel, and followed the boys. Otis eased the car up slowly, trailing the boys in the night shadows.

The head boy pulled into the driveway of a country-style house with a manicured lawn and perfectly

trimmed trees. Billy dropped his bike on the grass and ran inside.

Otis cut the engine, and the car drifted to a stop in front of the house. The cows tiptoed across the lawn and crouched near some shrubs outside the boy's first-floor bedroom.

"Now remember, honey," his mother said, attempting to reprimand her son. "I told you, you can't be staying out this late on a school night." Otis peeked through the bedroom window.

"Oh, we can't be staying out late or blah, blah dee blah, blah," Willy responded. "Whatever. I'll do what I want, when I want, 'cause I want to do it! Yeeeah!" With that, his mother backed slowly out of his room to avoid any more outbursts.

He hopped into his bed and fluffed up his pillow. Willy grabbed his stuffed sock monkey and pulled it close. "You've come to the wrong place, monkey." He hurled the stuffed animal against the wall. "Yeeeah!"

Willy lay back on his bed, remembering his fun evening in the meadow. His eyes closed, and he drifted off to sleep.

"He's asleep," Otis whispered to the others. He pressed his hooves against the window. It slowly slid open.

"Shhh," Otis said. "Here we go." He rolled over the windowsill and landed on the bedroom floor. He gave a helping hoof to Eddy and Igg while Bud stood watch outside.

They crept to the bed and pressed their hooves gently against the boy's body.

"On three," Otis instructed. "One . . . two . . . three! Moo!"

The cows shoved the boy. He slid across the mattress and crashed to the floor. When he landed he looked up, frantic and startled. Three large cows stood on their hind legs and glared at him.

"That's called boy tipping!" Otis laughed. "Ha, ha, ha!"

The boy screamed, louder than he had ever screamed before. His parents rushed down the hall. Eddy dove through the bedroom window. Igg followed, but his hind end jammed in the frame. Otis head-butted Igg free, popping the large cow out. Otis dove after him. They raced across the lawn and got back into the Beadys' little car.

"Let's get out of here," the cows yelled frantically. "Oh, oh boy. Come on, hurry up!"

The boy sat on the floor, horrified, clutching his sock monkey and rocking back and forth. "Never go to

the meadows," he repeated. "Never go to the meadows. Never go to the meadows. Treat cows nicely. Never go to the meadows."

Willy's mom and dad burst into their son's room and stared at him. "No more TV for you," his dad said. Then he looked at his wife, "And we're cutting out the energy drinks."

Sixteen

"Put crowns on our heads, because we are the kings!" Eddy yelled. The car zoomed down the street, screeched around a corner, and left the housing development in its dust. Otis laughed. He clenched his hoof and shoulder-punched Igg.

"Whoo hoo, hoo!" Otis yelled.

"Did you see his face?" Igg asked.

"Oh yeah," Eddy agreed.

"Price . . . ," Igg said.

"Less!" Bud finished.

Otis raised a bottle of milk in the air. "A toast!" he shouted. "To a new world order! We are calling the shots now!"

The Jersey cows held up their milk bottles and clinked them together. "Yeah! New world order," they chanted together.

"Nothing can touch us!" Otis exclaimed.

"Uh, Otis?" Eddy looked in the rearview mirror. The happiness fell from his face.

Red-and-blue lights were flashing behind them. A siren was blaring from the pursuing car. "Pull over to the side of the road!" a police officer yelled from a loudspeaker.

Otis's eyes widened in shock. "It's the cops!"

The Jersey cows panicked. "Oh man, oh man!"

"Let me out," Bud demanded. "You gotta let me out!"

"We can't pull over," Otis replied. "Hang on." Otis brought his hoof over the divider in the front seat and stomped it on the gas pedal, and the car rocketed off. Eddy gripped the steering wheel tighter, struggling to keep the car on the road as Otis pounded the gas. "What could be worse than this?"

Inside the police car the officer was sitting next to a cameraman. They were taping a live broadcast of *Cops on Patrol* for television.

The cameraman zoomed in for a close-up of Officer O'Hanlon. "What we got here's probably some teenagers going out for a joyride in their mom's car," O'Hanlon said to the camera. "We'll shake 'em up a bit, then send 'em home." He shook his head as if this happened all the time. "You know kids. Nothing a little pat down won't cure!" He laughed at his own joke. "That thing still on?"

"Is that a camera?" Otis spun around and looked into the police car behind them. "There's a camera in there!" Otis quickly realized what was going on. "They're taping *Cops on Patrol*!"

"Mommy!" Eddy yelled out. "Mooo-mmmy!"

"Okay, relax," Otis said calmly. "We can lose them. I mean, it's just one car, right?"

A police helicopter rose up beside them and swooped overhead. Its spotlight beamed down on the roof of the car.

"It's a chopper, it's a chopper!" Eddy yelled. "We're gonna die!"

Seventeen

"The police appear to be pursuing a late-model sedan.
. . ." Mrs. Beady put down her knitting and stared at
the late-night news. Mr. Beady dozed in his chair. The
TV showed a picture of the local police chasing after
a small car.

"Would you look at that?" Mrs. Beady said to her
snoring husband. "The world is going crazy. These
kids get all hopped up on diet soda and candy bars
and just—hey! That's our car!"

Mr. Beady woke up and squinted at the television.

He shook his head and took a sip of his drink.

Mrs. Beady pointed at the TV set. "That was a hoof! There's a cow in our car, and that is a hoof!" She ran to the telephone and punched in 9-1-1.

"Yes, operator, this is Nora Beady," she said into the telephone. There was a long pause. "What do you mean, what now? My car is on TV, and I think there's a cow in it! And I saw a cow outside my window. I think they may be linked!"

The phone went dead. The 9-1-1 operator had hung up on Mrs. Beady. Mr. Beady smiled and closed his eyes.

"Don't think I can't call again, Gary!" she yelled into the silent phone.

Otis glanced into the rearview mirror. Several police cars had joined in the chase, following closely behind the first car. "That's nice," Otis deadpanned. "Good."

Eddy started to panic. "They're going to catch us. They're going to dissect us. . . ."

"Quiet!" Otis needed a plan. He couldn't lead them back to the barnyard or let the cops catch them. He scanned the road ahead. They were coming to a wooded area. Otis lunged for the wheel and yanked it

hard to the right. "We're ditchin' out!"

"Holy moly!" cried Eddy.

"Hey, oh!" Igg gasped.

"Ow! Hey!" Bud added.

The Jersey cows screamed as Otis veered the car off the road. He yanked the wheel left, then right, then left again, weaving around the thick trees as Eddy floored the gas even harder. The car bounced over shrubs and bushes, spinning mud and rocks behind its wheels.

"Two all-beef patties," Eddy cried. "That's our future!"

The car skidded down a hill toward the woods. The police cars followed. Otis scraped the car past a row of the pine trees, but didn't see the thick bushes ahead. The car slammed into them, jerking to a stop. The cows were fine, but the car wasn't going any farther. Steam puffed from under the hood.

The four cows flung open the doors and exploded out of the crumpled car.

"Run!" Eddy yelled. "Run!"

Side by side, they sprinted through the woods. "I'm chaffing!" Otis cried. Flashlight beams cut through the trees, silhouetting the fugitives.

"I'll never do it again!" Eddy promised. "Never again!"

"We're coming up to a clearing," Otis said. "Follow my lead!"

The police helicopter circled the trees. Its spotlight danced on the ground, looking for the suspects. Officer O'Hanlon and the TV cameraman raced through the woods after the perpetrators. "They're making a run for it! Let's go!" Other police officers swarmed behind him like bees to honey.

Through the trees ahead of him, O'Hanlon heard the crunch of feet racing over the ground. His flashlight caught their shadows against the trees. "Geez, these guys are really big."

The cows burst from the woods into the clearing. No hiding places. Only a pleasant green meadow.

The police were getting closer. Their bright flashlights cut through the woods.

"Hurry up, boys!" O'Hanlon yelled. "They're right over here!" The police and the cameraman rushed out of the woods and into the clearing. "We got 'em now. Wha—?!" O'Hanlon exclaimed.

O'Hanlon scanned the grass. His suspects had disappeared. There were just four cows, standing on all fours and sleeping peacefully in the tall green grass of a pleasant meadow. O'Hanlon's flashlight beam shook in Otis's face. The cow pretended to wake

up. He opened his eyes halfway and stared at Officer O'Hanlon. "Hmmooo?" he said sleepily.

Eddy raised his head and let out a gentle mooo too.

O'Hanlon looked into the camera and smiled sheepishly. "Cows," he muttered. Out of breath he hunched over, wheezing for air. "Whooo, okay, so, they got lucky this time."

The helicopter's spotlight turned off. The craft pulled out and disappeared into the evening sky. The cops and the cameraman turned toward the woods and trudged back to their cars.

"Mooo," Otis said quietly. He watched O'Hanlon disappear into the night.

Eighteen

"Could you guys believe that?" Eddy said. "Did you guys see me? Me? I am fearless, baby. Fearless!"

"Oh, yeah," said Igg. "Fear-"

"Less, huh." Otis simply rolled his eyes.

"This thing's heavier than I thought," Bud complained as the four of them pushed the beat-up car back down the dirt road.

"I think it rolled over my foot," Eddy whined.

Otis and the Jersey cows pushed Mrs. Beady's battered car up the driveway and toward her farmhouse.

Branches poked out from the broken windows. The hood was crumpled. The fender was twisted like a pretzel. Deep scratches ran across the length of the car.

"It looks good," Bud observed. The car rolled to a stop outside the front door. The cows snuck down the driveway, heading for home. The driver's-side door dropped from its hinges and clattered to the ground.

"We left it the same way we found it," Eddy said.

Soon the cows were back in the field, laughing uncontrollably at their good fortune. There were high fives and cheers all around. Tonight had been their greatest adventure ever.

"Toodle doo, Otis!" Eddy laughed. "Same time tomorrow night, huh? Hey guys, can you imagine Ben doing something like that?" Eddy asked.

"No way!" Bud giggled, and the three Jersey cows laughed all the way out into the fields. The Jersey cows laughed, but Otis realized that Eddy was right— Ben never would have behaved so irresponsibly. He never would have put their safety at risk as Otis had. An overwhelming sadness swept over Otis as he remembered his father and what he had sacrificed to protect the barnyard. What would his father have thought of his behavior? Otis knew he would have been disappointed, again.

Nineteen

Otis sighed and began to make his way to his father's lookout spot, where he sat watch.

Waiting for something to happen was the ultimate in boredom. He'd been standing watch for almost fifteen minutes and already wanted to do something else. Anything else. The still night air was peaceful. The farmer had gone to bed, still nursing his painful headache. Music echoed from the barn. Otis could hear the distant clatter of dancing hooves and fun-loving party animals. There was another hoedown tonight. Otis knew what he

was missing and sighed again. Pip lay on his back on top of Otis's head, staring at the barn and sighing loudly.

"Explain to me exactly why we are doing this?" Pip asked.

"Because it's what my dad would do," Otis replied. "Why don't you go have fun, Pip?" Otis suggested. "I can do this on my own."

"No way, we're homeboys," Pip stated. "I'm here with you."

"Really, it's all right."

"Okay!" Pip shot off Otis's head like a ball from a cannon. "I'll bring you back a snack or something. Later, okay! Be back—hey whoo hoo, hoo!" He ran through the field in a straight line directly toward the barn as fast as his tiny legs could carry him.

Otis watched his friend disappear, wishing he could be with him. He knew his place was here, tonight. He was in charge now.

"Okay, I'm alert." Otis sighed. Off in the distance a coyote's howl cut through the calm. A shiver went up Otis's spine. He leaned forward to get a closer look at what was in the distance. He saw nothing. "Come on back," he muttered. "I'm right here."

"Mind if I join you?" a girl's voice said from behind him. It was Daisy.

"No, I mean, sure, I . . . ," Otis stammered. "I no mind you—Jeez . . . I can't even talk to you. Hang on a second."

Otis scampered away. He returned in seconds, dragging two wooden chaise lounges behind him. He reached a hoof to help her into one of the chairs. "Here you go, just let me . . ."

"No, I can still sit on my own. I think," she said. She deftly maneuvered her pregnant body into the chaise lounge and made herself comfortable. She rubbed her protruding stomach and gasped. "Oh my gosh!" she exclaimed. "Oh my gosh! The baby's coming!"

"What?" Otis's eyes almost popped from his head.

Daisy laughed. "Made you jump."

"Nice. Thank you." Otis pouted. He slumped back into his chair. "I almost swallowed my cud."

"It's beautiful, isn't it?"

"My cud?" Otis said, confused.

"The night."

Otis looked up at the stars in the sky. "Oh, yeah, that too. Nice. My dad had a thing about stars."

"Tell me, what was he like?" Daisy asked.

"My pop? He was amazing," Otis began proudly. "Bigger than life, you know. Funny, we're not even related. He found me and took me in. I never thought

about it before, but everything he did was for me. He's the only family I've ever known. The last time we talked he told me that the night he found me he looked up into the sky, and he said that the stars . . ." Otis paused. Memories of his dad flooded back into Otis's head. This was the first time he'd talked about his dad since he passed away. He was glad Daisy had asked. "I miss him," Otis said. Then he quickly changed gears. "And what about you?" Otis continued. "You know, I mean if that's too personal, and if I'm overstepping, like, a boundary or . . . you know what, too bad. Cough it up."

Daisy laughed. "Okay, well, where do I start? I was married, and life was good. It seems like forever ago now, but one day a bad storm rolled in. Bessy and I were in the meadow and we found a place on high ground. But when we went home, well . . . everyone was gone."

"You know what I think?" Otis said, trying to lighten the mood. "I think some good things are going to start happening to you and me."

Otis leaned back on his chaise lounge. He reached for Daisy's hoof and held on to it, giving it a gentle squeeze.

Twenty

A small rabbit gnawed on a tree root poking through the ground. He stopped, midchew. Something rustled in the trees. A shadow flickered near a bush. Trouble was coming. The rabbit's eyes darted from side to side. His heart pounded in his furry chest. He bolted, racing through the meadow.

A coyote leaped from the trees in pursuit, bearing down on the rabbit. The rabbit zigged and zagged through the meadow. His quick movements surprised the coyote. The rabbit gained a few steps, hopped over

a rotten log laying across the field, and cut through a small opening in a pile of rocks.

A second coyote raced from the woods and joined the chase. Then a third. The rabbit spotted a hole in the distance and ran for it. The coyotes yipped in anticipation.

The coyotes' premature celebrations woke Otis from his slumber. His eyes snapped open and focused on the rabbit. He saw the coyotes closing in. He jumped off the chaise lounge and hopped the fence. The noise woke Daisy.

The rabbit made it to the hole and dove in. Safe—for now. The coyotes surrounded the tiny opening. They growled and yipped into it. They thrust their paws into the hole and dug, throwing dirt behind them. The rabbit wasn't getting away.

Suddenly one of the coyotes was pulled away from the hole. It yelped in pain and fell to the ground. Dag lifted his snout from the rabbit hole. Who would dare?!

Then Otis came into view. Dag snarled and stared, his eyes narrow slits of anger, his teeth dripped saliva. He stood up on his hind legs.

Dag growled. "What do you want to be? A hero, cow?"

Otis skidded to a stop. The other coyotes fanned out and circled him. They snarled their teeth and nipped at his hooves.

Otis lunged at Dag. Another coyote sideswiped him, knocking Otis off balance. A second coyote bit the cow's tail. Otis turned to swat it at him. He missed and landed face-first into the dirt. The coyotes continued to circle him, growling and snarling and drooling. There were too many of them for Otis to handle on his own. Dag's eyes narrowed. Something in the way this cow moved reminded him of something . . . or someone.

"Hey, you're Ben's kid. Otis, right?" Dag said. There was an evil twinkle in the coyote's eye. "I'm Dag. Sorry about your dad." Dag gave Otis a mischievous grin and began to smile. "Tragic. Wanna go see him?"

Dag and his pack laughed. Otis lunged at Dag, but a coyote chomped down on his tail. Otis cried out and spun around. The other coyotes snapped and yipped at him.

"So, they left you in charge?" Dag laughed. "Oh, *that's* precious. You thought you could fill Ben's shoes? Otis, where were you? Were you off having fun, laughing with your barnyard buddies? You could have made a difference had you been there for him, but you

weren't, were you? That's your life, no difference." Dag paced around Otis. A plan was forming in the coyote's head. It was a plan that would make life easier for his pack. "Okay," he announced. "From here on out this is the way it's gonna work. We show up, you look the other way. A few animals missing here and there . . . hey, it's the natural order of things."

Dag leaned in. Otis could smell his foul breath. Otis staggered back a step, too scared to fight or say anything. The other coyotes continued to circle him, lunging forward and snapping their teeth.

"It'll be our little secret," Dag said. "Oh, and Ben's kid, if you should think about getting a sudden burst of courage, we'll take every animal in sight. Now go back and make everyone feel safe. We'll be seeing you tomorrow night. That's a date." He snapped his teeth at Otis to offer one final warning. "See you round." Dag threw his head back with laughter. "Round? You're fat."

Dag and his pack ran off into the night. He stopped atop a small hill and howled to the moon. Otis shivered as a chill shot up his spine, and he slowly headed back to the barnyard.

Twenty-One

"Hey, Pop. I wanted to come by and . . . look, you were a great dad."

Otis sat at his father's grave. He had done a lot of thinking since he'd said good-bye to the Jersey cows. "I mean, I don't know what I was thinking," Otis continued. "For a minute I actually thought I could take your place. But those coyotes. You would have stood up to them. You wouldn't have backed down. I was so afraid tonight. I know I always said I wasn't you, and I'm not. But I wish I was." Otis hung his head

sadly. Tears rolled down his cheeks. "I can't do it, Pop. I gotta go. I'm sorry."

Otis walked away, his head low. He headed back to the barnyard to pack up his things.

Twenty-Two

"And Duke will handle things, and everything will be fine," Otis said to Pip, almost in a whisper. He headed toward the barn as Pip ran after him.

It was morning now, and Otis had been up most of the night. He had made a decision, and he wasn't going to change his mind.

"Wait! What are you talking about?" Pip demanded.

"Could you just not say anything?" Otis waved at Pip to be quiet. "I don't want to make a big thing about this."

"Hey, everybody!" Pip yelled as loud as his little lungs would let him. "Otis is leaving the barnyard!"

Otis shot an unhappy glance to Pip and continued walking to the barn. The mouse shrugged. Peck, Pig, Freddy, and dozens of other animals ran to Otis and bombarded him with questions.

"What? Is this a joke?"

"Leaving?"

"Was it something we said?"

"You're kidding, right?"

"Why?"

Pip scrambled up the doorway and stood eye to eye with Otis.

"Oat, seriously, you and me, we're like best friends—"

"No, Pip, it's over," Otis interrupted. He turned to the animals behind him. "I'm leaving, all right? No big whoop. Continue on with your day."

"Come on, Otis," Peck said. "We'll do what you say."

"That's the point," Otis explained. "I don't want you to do what I say. I don't want any of you to have to listen to me."

Freddy slapped his paws over his ears. "Don't listen to him!"

The others covered their ears too.

"Stop doing what I say!" Otis ordered.

Everyone immediately uncovered their ears.

"Okay, so what you're saying is that you'll stay if we don't do what you say?" Pig asked.

Otis stared at Pig. A bee was stuck in Pig's snout. "Dead bee," Otis answered.

Pig blew his nose. "Thanks." The bee shot out and buzzed away. "Again, alive."

Duke stuck his head through the crowd. "Duke, you're in charge now," Otis stated. "Get the other dogs together. You guys can handle things better than I ever could."

"Sure, Otis, if you say so." Duke wanted to be in charge, but not this way. He didn't want Otis to leave. No one did.

"I've got my own life to lead. I don't belong here anymore." Otis turned from the group and shuffled into the barn. The animals weren't sure what to say or do. One by one, they retreated to the barnyard, their heads hung low, unanswered questions floating in their minds.

Only Pip remained. He watched his buddy for a long time, and then sadly he turned away.

Inside the barn Otis packed a few of his favorite

things into a burlap bag. Daisy walked into the barn and stood behind him. "What happened, Otis?" Otis started to reply, but Daisy held up a hoof in front of his face. "And please don't say nothing."

Otis sighed. "Look, it's complicated."

"If you're hurting, let me help," she pleaded. "I'd like to help."

Daisy stared at Otis. She didn't understand. She touched his hoof and gave it a gentle squeeze. Otis looked up from his packing and saw the sadness in her eyes. He had to tell her the truth. She deserved at least that much.

"You want to know what happened?" he asked. "I froze, okay? Last night I didn't run off the coyotes. I couldn't do anything. Now, they're going to come back tonight, and I can't protect anyone. Everyone here trusts me, and I can't protect a single one of them."

Daisy rested a hoof on Otis's shoulder. "Otis, the best leader isn't the biggest or the strongest. The best leader is the one who cares the most."

Otis sighed. "Yeah, that's a nice thought, Daisy. That's a really nice thought." Otis continued packing. "I'll tell you one thing. I'm really gonna miss Bessy."

Daisy laughed. As sad as she was, Otis could still make her smile. "Okay, if this is what you have to do,

I understand," Daisy said. "But I just want you to know one thing . . . even if you do leave, I believe in you." She leaned forward and kissed him. She turned and walked away from the barn, tears filling her eyes.

Otis watched her go, choking back his own tears. He wanted to stay, but he knew he couldn't. He couldn't be his father. He couldn't protect his friends. He'd tried it once and failed.

Otis tied a knot in his burlap bag and threw it over his shoulder. He stepped into the barnyard. No one was around. It was like they'd run away too. Otis took a final look around: the barn, the farmer's house, the pigpen, and the meadow. He sighed and headed to the gate.

"Otis! Otis!" Peck came running from the henhouse. His wings flapped frantically.

"All right, Peck, take it easy," Otis said. He leaned down to the rooster's height. "What's the matter?"

Peck was out of breath. He could barely squeak out the words. "They took—they took—we gotta . . . come on!" Peck led the way. Otis ran after him, fearful of what terrible thing Peck was leading him to.

The animals were gathered around the henhouse. A mixed feeling of fear and sadness filled the air. Their faces told the whole story. Something was wrong—terribly, terribly wrong.

"Otis, the coyotes," Duke explained. "It just happened. They took Etta, Hanna, maybe six or seven others. I don't know." Duke shook his head. "They've never come during the day before."

"They knew I wouldn't be expecting them until tonight," Otis muttered. "They played me."

"What?" Duke queried.

"Nothing," Otis answered.

"Otis . . . they took Maddy," Daisy said.

This news hit Otis hard. His eyes widened. His stomach felt as if he'd been punched. Maddy was just a chick. Only one thing could make even a coyote take a cute little chick like Maddy: pure evil.

"Those coyotes are strong, Otis." Miles leaned against the side of the henhouse. "I was just wondering what a stronger man might do."

Otis thought for a moment. He saw the look of fear in the other animals' eyes. Fear of the coyotes. Fear of what would happen next, of who would be taken next. Otis had lost his father to the coyotes. He couldn't afford to lose his friends, too. He handed his burlap sack to Miles. "You'll look after things?"

"Be proud to," Miles said.

"I'll be back." Otis turned and walked across the barnyard. He knew where he had to go. He knew what

had to be done. This was not the time to run away. This was the time to be the stronger man.

Pip raced after his friend. He hopped onto Otis's leg and scampered up his back to rest on his shoulder. "I'm going too."

"No, Pip, stay here," Otis commanded. He said nothing more, but Pip could tell from Otis's voice that he was serious. Otis picked Pip off his shoulder and set him down in a tree. He hopped the fence and was outside the perimeter.

"You can't do this alone," Pip called after him. "They could kill you!"

"Yeah, I guess they could." Otis didn't look back. He was headed for the distant rocky hills toward an old abandoned junkyard.

He was headed straight for the coyotes' den.

Twenty-Three

The sun was setting, a deep red disk, fading behind the hills. Long shadows crept across the junkyard. Tractors, balers, combines, and other broken farm equipment outlined the edges, creating a skyline of sharp points and jagged edges. Etta, Hanna, Maddy, and the other hens were standing on a tree trunk, bound together with twine.

A coyote squatted next to them, adding more wood to an already large fire.

Dag leaned comfortably against a rock, filing his

fangs to merciless points. He smiled as the sun set slowly. It was almost dinnertime. "It's nice of you ladies to join us this evening," he taunted. "Thank you for being so patient, but we prefer dining at night." He howled with hungry delight. The other coyotes joined in.

"You're a wonderful species," Dag continued. "I love chicken. My favorite part is the skin."

"You're a big meaner," Maddy squeaked.

"What?" Dag asked.

"You're a meaner," Maddy said.

"Meaner, meaner," Dag mocked. He leaned in close to the cute little chick, his jaws open wide. Saliva dripped from his sharpened teeth. "Meaners gotta eat too." He snapped his jaws shut. Maddy jumped.

"Leave her alone!" Etta yelled.

Dag pointed at Etta. "This one's mine," he said to the other coyotes. "Cook her while I have the little one for an appetizer. Because I'm a meaner." Dag yanked Maddy from the group. Maddy squirmed as Dag lowered her into his mouth.

"Put the chick down, Dag."

Dag and the other coyotes turned to see Otis standing in front of them, his back against the sunset. Surprise registered on Dag's face. This was the first time anyone had come to *their* lair, the first time

anyone had invaded *their* home. Dag nodded to his pack. They stood on all fours, digging their paws into the ground. Growling and snarling, they bared their razor-sharp teeth. The hair on the back of their necks stood at attention. They were ready to attack. All they needed was a sign from Dag.

Otis didn't flinch.

"Otis," Etta said, relieved.

"Oaty!" Maddy yelled.

Dag grinned at Otis. "We suddenly got a burst of courage, did we?"

Otis kept a watchful eye. They could not be trusted. He remembered that from their last encounter. "You know, I didn't come to chat. I came for the hens."

"That's not gonna work, Oaty, *oatay*? Because we're eating them for dinner," Dag retorted angrily.

"Okay, all right, well, first, what I'm going to do is, I'm going to take that chick from you," Otis said firmly. "Then, while you're still picking yourself off the ground, I'm going to gather up the rest of the hens, and I'm going to leave."

"And exactly how do you propose to do that?" Dag snarled.

Otis stepped forward and grabbed Dag by the neck and threw him onto a pile of junk. Maddy popped out

of Dag's paw and lunged into the air. Otis reached out and caught her. Otis smiled at Maddy and placed her with the other hens.

"Kill him!" Dag seethed as dozens of coyotes came out of the woodwork to attack.

They lunged at Otis, snapping and gnawing. Otis grabbed one by the tail and hurled it into two other coyotes. All three fell to the ground in a heap. A coyote jumped on Otis's back. Otis flipped him over to the ground. The coyotes kept coming from all sides. Otis lost count. As soon as he saw one, he swung and kept swinging. He jabbed one with his left hoof and sent it flying backward. Otis punched another with his right hoof and knocked him unconscious. A coyote lunged at his head, and Otis ducked. The coyote crashed into another and fell down. Otis had the upper hoof. He taunted the coyotes. "MOOO!"

Dag snuck around Otis's back, watching him and waiting for the right moment to strike, just like he had with Ben. Otis held a coyote over his head and threw him into the junkyard. Dag seized his chance and lunged at Otis and bit his leg, hard.

It was the same move that had brought his dad down. Otis howled in agony and dropped to one knee. Thoughts of his dad flashed into his head. Was this

how it had ended for him? Was this how Dag had cheated Otis out of his father? The coyotes swarmed Otis, and he disappeared under a mountain of yipping, biting, snarling creatures.

"That should do," Dag ordered.

The coyotes backed away. Otis was on his knees, beaten and weak. His chest heaved with each agonizing breath.

"Well, look at the hero," Dag teased. "You thought you could come here into *my* den." Dag leaned close and whispered into Otis's ear. "Now, why don't you lay there and watch while we eat your friends."

He heard Dag's cruel laughter. Otis pushed the pain from his mind. Suddenly he didn't care about his own survival. He was his friends' only hope. And maybe he was the barnyard's only hope as well. "A strong man stands up for himself. A stronger man stands up for others," he said, finally understanding what those words really meant. He had to save his friends. Nothing else mattered.

"This should be fun," Dag said with delight.

Otis brought himself to his feet. He towered over the coyotes. They cautiously backed away. A stab of uncertainty cut through Dag's wicked laugh. The coyote fell silent.

Courage swelled through Otis's limbs. Dag's eyes widened. Otis might prove a worthy adversary after all. Dag smiled. He sniffed the air, and his smile faded. He turned around.

Miles stood on the hillside overlooking the junkyard. Pip, Pig, Freddy, and Peck were next to him. Otis saw them too and smiled.

"I smell fear," Dag said dismissively.

"I told you they could smell it!" Peck cried.

"They can smell it?" Freddy yelled, outraged. Then he sniffed himself quickly. "Oh yeah, I have it. A lot of it."

"Just stick together and you'll be all right," Miles assured them all.

"Yeah," agreed Freddy, day dreaming about Peck again. "I'll watch your juicy back, uh, I mean, your regular back," Freddy corrected himself. Pip stood on Pig's head, surveying the junkyard. He saw Otis down below. "Hey!" Pig felt something dropping on his head.

"Sorry, man," Pip apologized. "They're just pellets. I'm nervous."

Twenty-Four

"That's your army?" Dag asked mockingly.

"Something tells me you may want to take a couple of steps back," Otis announced. Instantly, a low rumble started to build. Dag looked back and forth, trying to locate where the sound was coming from. Then he realized it was coming from atop the big hill of junk. An ominous light glimmered, then grew more visible. *WHAM!* Smashing through a wall of junk, Mrs. Beady's car roared up and over the hill.

The Jersey cows leaned out of the windows.

"Moo hooo, hooo!" Eddy yelled with excitement.

Igg yelled, "Here comes trou . . ."

"Ble!" Bud finished.

"Trou . . ."

"Bull!"

"Trou . . ."

"BULL!"

Meanwhile, on the top of the hill, Otis's crew was psyching themselves up for the plunge.

"Me too," Pig replied. "Talk me into it, Pip. Talk me into it."

"Okay, flip your lip a little bit," Pip said. "I wanna see that angry face! Make me scared! You're mad! You're a pig, and you're mad. . . ."

"Let's do this!" Pig yelled. He charged down the hill at full speed, screaming his tribal victory chant at the top of his lungs. "AAAHHHIII!" Suddenly, he tripped and sailed forward, smashing into a huge pile of junk. He bounced off car hooks and a washing machine, landing finally at the feet of two angry coyotes and knocking his elbow in the process. Pig wallowed over them. "Oo, oo, ow, my elbow," he yelled. "Ooo, aaah!"

Pip leaped off Pig's head and dove onto a coyote's shoulder. The coyote snapped at Pip, ready to bite him. "You know what I'm going to do? I'm going to go right

in your ear!" Pip jumped and disappeared into the coyote's ear.

The coyote freaked. He screamed and hopped around trying to shake Pip out. "There's a mouse in my ear! A mouse in my ear!" The coyote ran away. Pip jumped out and landed on the ground.

"That's one for me!" Pip squeaked.

Down below, the Jersey cows were doing some damage. Igg and Bud whacked several of them with sticks as they zoomed by. Eddy turned the wheel wildly, trying to knock over as many coyotes as he could. The car careened out of control. It skidded across the junkyard and crashed into a heap. The Jersey cows kicked open the doors and barreled out.

Several coyotes rushed toward them. The Jersey cows bent over like bulls and charged into them, galloping hard in a stampede. Their heads butted the coyotes, tossing them into the air.

Dag backed away and snuck into an old school bus. Safe and hidden, he watched from inside.

Coyotes scattered around the junkyard. Otis extended his arms and clothes lined two of them. They crashed to the ground. Otis picked them up.

"So sorry," he said. "Here, let me give you a hand." He slammed the two of them together. The coyotes

slid out of Otis's hooves and piled on the ground.

"Yeah!" Maddy cheered. She swung her feathered fists through the air, offering encouragement to Otis. "You show them, Oaty!"

A coyote rushed toward the hens. Peck jumped onto the coyote's back and pecked him as if he were fresh chicken feed. The coyote reached around and gripped Peck. He brought the rooster to his waiting jaws.

Whack!

Freddy jumped up and bashed the coyote with his tail. The coyote fell backward into a pile of junk. "Nobody . . . eats . . . my . . . tasty . . . friend!" Freddy yelled. "Except me. But only if he lets me!" Then Freddy grabbed the coyote's arm and bit down—hard! Suddenly, Freddy's eyes widened and an expression of glee spread over his face. He licked his lips. He couldn't believe what he tasted. "It tastes like chicken!" he cried out with excitement. "Chicken! Chick-chick chicky-chick chicken!" he yelled, chasing after them as they scattered through the yard.

Coyotes moved closer to Otis. He pulled out his cell phone and dialed quickly. The coyotes growled and snarled. Otis could feel their hot breath. He spoke quickly into the phone. "We're ready, Gopher!"

Instantly holes opened up in the g... Otis. The startled coyotes stopped and yipped in shock. Dozens of gophers popped from the holes. They kicked and punched the stunned coyotes, and then dropped back into the holes as quickly as they'd emerged. The confused coyotes swung wildly and repeatedly into the air. The gophers were too fast for them. The pack dropped to the ground, exhausted.

At the edge of the junkyard, Miles was watching the battle, when suddenly four coyotes began closing in on him. "Well, well. Whatever will I do?" Miles asked, not the least bit concerned. In a flash of light his famous kicking leg knocked not one, not two, but three coyotes down and out. A lone coyote stood there, stunned.

"I got something special for you," Miles said. A small, very familiar, wooden crate lay next to Miles's feet. It began to shake and rattle. Miles kicked the latch from the box. The door fell open, and Wild Mike roared out. The coyote was startled. Wild Mike chased the coyote out of the junkyard and into the night, its yips and howls fading into the darkness.

"I love that little guy." Miles chuckled. "Go get him, Mikey."

The beaten coyotes scurried from the junkyard. Otis pounded the last few and chased them away. He

Dag's moment had ... out of the bus and stalked ... unsuspecting Otis. This time he'd ... big, dumb cow who was boss. He'd make ... pay for his boldness, just like he had made Ben pay. He was careful to stay behind Otis and out of his sight.

"Oteeezz!" Pip saw Dag approach his friend. "Hey, Otis!" Pip yelled. "Behind you, watch out!"

Pig, Peck, and Freddy joined in, yelling at Otis. But he was too far away from them to hear. They had only one option left. "Peck, it's up to you!" Freddy said. "We need a crow, and we need it now!"

Peck knew what he had to do. He cleared his throat and threw back his head.

Dag opened his mouth and crouched, like a coiled spring. Suddenly he launched himself at Otis.

Peck squealed out his crow call with wild abandon. Otis heard it and turned around just in time to see Dag leaping toward him. Otis gripped Dag by the throat. "Remember me?" Otis said. "I'm Ben's kid." Otis slammed the coyote against the side of an old, rusty tractor and held him there, keeping a grip on Dag's neck. He raised his other hoof and curled it into a powerful fist. He took a deep breath and caught

himself. *What would Dad have done?* Otis thought. He leaned close to Dag and glared into his eyes.

Dag was beaten. The growls and snarls were long gone. A little whimper shot out from his throat. Otis was the stronger man now. He knew what to do.

"Never come back," Otis warned.

Dag swallowed hard and nodded. Otis threw him to the ground. Dag crumpled. He had lost everything, and all because of some chickens and a cow.

"Pip?" Otis asked his friend. "What do you think I should use with this one?"

"I'd go with the iron, man," Pip replied.

Eddy flipped a piece of metal to Otis. Otis squared up like a golfer and swung the metal bar. The bar smacked Dag in his butt. The coyote howled and hurtled over a large pile of junk. He ricocheted off an old washing machine and plopped to the ground. Dag pulled himself up and limped off into the night.

Freddy, Peck, Pip, and the others rejoiced in their victory.

The coyotes were defeated. Otis stood in the center of the junkyard and watched the last of the coyotes skulk away. This was the final coyote season, and he knew they'd never return. Maddy, the hens, and all the barnyard animals were safe—now and forever.

Otis reached out to hug and thank all of his friends.

But they were the ones who were grateful.

Otis rubbed his sore shoulder and shook the stiffness from his left leg. He needed a nice relaxing swim in the pond. But he knew the pond was for drinking, not for swimming.

Miles nodded knowingly. They had made the right choice after all.

Pip climbed on top of Otis's head. Otis picked up Maddy and put her up there too.

"Quite a night, huh?" Pip said, pleased with himself. "We took down the coyotes, Peck learned to crow, and by the time we get back we'll have a new member of the barnyard running around."

"Huh?" Otis said.

"Daisy," Pip explained. "She, like, went into labor just after you left."

Etta and Hanna shrieked with joy. Etta spurted out an egg, and Hanna clucked wildly.

"Daisy's . . . ," Otis stammered, lost for words.

"She's having her baby, dude," Pip said. "What did you think was going to happen? She would just keep getting bigger or something?"

"Wha—? Is she all right?" Otis asked a million questions. "I . . . I . . . we've . . . we've gotta get back!"

"It's doubtful we'll make it back on time walking," Miles said. "I'm sure she's gonna be all right, Otis."

"Miles, I've got to be there," Otis pleaded.

Miles thought for a second, then smiled.

It was nighttime at the truck stop. Otis crept past the eighteen-wheelers, the moving vans, and the SUVs. He was headed straight for the row of motorcycles that lined the parking lot.

"We can call and tell them where to pick the bikes up," Miles said with a smile.

Otis sped in front of the others, feeling the wind pressing against his hide. He had to get home to Daisy.

Forget about walking, Otis thought. This was the only way to travel. They burned rubber down the road, a motorcycle caravan of cows and chickens, a mule, a ferret, a rooster, a pig, and a mouse. Together they owned the road and ruled the night.

Twenty-Five

It was quiet inside the barn. The pigs, goats, chickens, cows, horses, and sheep were waiting patiently outside. Duke was pacing nervously. Otis roared into the barnyard on his borrowed motorcycle and skidded to a stop. He hopped off and raced to Duke.

"Duke, what's happening?" he asked urgently.

"Otis, you know. Come on." Duke fumbled for words. "I think, I'm pretty sure. It's . . . yeah, it's time."

Otis rushed into the barn. Daisy lay in the hay inside the first stall. Bessy sat by her side, holding her hoof. Daisy saw Otis and smiled. Otis ran to the stall and dropped next to her.

"Otis, I was so worried."

"Worried about what? I *so* had that covered." He smiled. "It's okay. I'm here."

Otis took Daisy's hoof. Bessy looked at him with surprised admiration. Pip scrambled up the side of a stall and stood on a slat, eye level with Bessy.

"And I'm here for you too."

Bessy glanced at Pip. She blew a puff of air from the side of her mouth and knocked Pip off the slat. He fell backward into the hay. Bessy turned her attention to Daisy. "Okay, girl, you're doing fine. Just breathe."

"Oooh." Daisy took deep breaths. The baby was coming. Pip, Pig, Freddy, Peck, Miles, and Duke gathered around the stall, wide-eyed.

"Man, that looks like it hurts," Pig observed.

"That's a very profound insight," Duke said sarcastically.

"Well, excuse me for being a pig."

"How come nothing's happening yet?" Pip asked.

Daisy followed her friend's instructions. Otis held her

125

hoof tighter. Seconds later Bessy held up the tiny calf.

"It's a beautiful little boy!" she exclaimed.

Daisy beamed. Otis looked at the baby calf with wonder. Bessy saw the look in Otis's eyes and handed him the baby. Otis cradled the newborn gently in his hooves. "He's perfect," Otis observed. "What are you gonna name him?"

"I was thinking that I kind of like . . . Ben," Daisy said.

Otis looked softly at Daisy, and tears welled up in his eyes. "Well, I think that's just great! Hey there, little Ben."

Otis set Ben on the ground. He stumbled and swayed along on his legs, making his way to his mother. Daisy opened her arms, and Ben tumbled into her hug. Otis knelt at Daisy's side and joined the embrace.

Duke led Otis's friends into the stall. As their spokesdog he stood at the front of the group. "Otis, we were all talking, and we know you may have other plans, we understand that, but we really, really appreciate what you did around here—coyotes and all. And, well, we were wondering if maybe you were planning on staying around a little longer?"

Otis stood and faced his friends. He took a deep breath, looking down at Daisy and little Ben. "I'll just say this: As long as I'm still kickin', no animal

126

will be harmed inside that fence!"

Daisy smiled. The other animals cheered. They high-fived Otis and slapped him on the back.

That night the energy in the barnyard was electric. This was more than just a hoedown; it was a celebration. The coyotes were gone. The barnyard had a new leader, and the new leader had a new son.

Otis shuffled across the dance floor, dancing with Daisy and little Ben until they were outside. He looked up into the sky and a smile came across his face. Just like Ben said, the stars always dance.

Mrs. Beady sat in front of her mirror and lathered on face cream.

"I, Nora Beady, am a precious object. I shall treat myself as such. Uh-huh!" She noticed her hair was wild and frizzy. "Oh, gosh, I wonder how I could have forgotten to use conditioner!"

Her hair twitched and shook. Two crazy eyeballs popped up through the tangles. Two legs bulged out the sides. Wild Mike started dancing on her scalp! She SCREAMED!

Out in the living room Mr. Beady changed the channel on the television and sighed.

THE END